Crossing the Arafura Sea

Also by Bruce Grant:

A Young Woman from China

The Last Kiss

Crossing the
Arafura Sea

BRUCE GRANT

Cover image of girl © iStock Photo
Background image © Stockvault

Cover Design and typeset by BookPOD Pty Ltd

Printed and bound in Australia by BookPOD Pty Ltd

Typeset in Garamond Premier Pro 12/15

Extract from *My People*, 4th Edition (ISBN 9790731407408 /
0731407407) by Oodgeroo Noonuccal and quotes from *Mendorong
Jack Kuntikunti* An English-Indonesian edition. Editors R.F. Brissenden
and Sapardi Djoko Damono. Publisher Yayasan Obor Indonesia.
© Reprinted with permission from John Wiley & Sons Ltd.

The poetry extracts from 'Woman to Man' from *A Human Pattern:
Selected Poems* (ISBN: 0195536509) by Judith Wright, ETT Imprint,
Sydney, 1996. © Reprinted with kind permission from ETT Imprint.

Extract from *La Figlia Che Piange* from T.S. Eliot: *The Complete Poems
and Plays* (ISBN: 9780571088577), Faber & Faber Ltd, 1969.
© Reprinted with permission from Faber & Faber Ltd.

A Catalogue-in-Publication is available from
the National Library of Australia

ISBN: 978-0-9925514-4-5
eISBN: 978-0-9925514-5-2

Part One

1

WHAT IS ENCHANTMENT? IS IT like power, measurable not in itself but by the effect it has, exhilarating, devastating? More insidious than infatuation, more potent than fascination? Is it like a perfume whose fragrance you can never forget, a melody that keeps returning? Or is it something you self-induce to justify the pursuit of pleasure, a secular bewitchment against which you pretend to struggle in vain? He did not ask himself these questions when he was enchanted, only afterwards.

She was an alert figure in a row of earnest faces. He found himself directing his talk to her. His distrust of the state and irritation with bureaucracy and red tape led him to embrace what he called "globalisation", by which he meant a new world order designed by free market forces, not governments. He noted that she was diligently writing in a notebook; he was pleased when she nodded in agreement with something he had said. When she became distracted, glancing about, he pulled his thoughts together and raised the level of his voice to bring her back.

When they were later introduced, she said, "I wonder if we are giving the wrong signals, trying to clasp hands across the Arafura Sea." She paused, allowing a humorous thought to form. "Perhaps we should just wave to each other." Her eyes darted at him over a half-formed smile. She spoke as if she did not quite believe what she was saying but was saying it anyhow, perhaps to test him. He said, "You wave to people you know." She said, "How can you be sure you know someone?" He replied, gravely, "I mean 'know' as being aware of, not in the biblical sense." "Oh," she said, in a lowered voice, as if she knew what he was getting at, and then smiled. Her smile was generous, promising honesty and laughter.

He assumed, from their conversation, she was Indonesian, but she might have been Italian or Bulgarian or Iranian. Her colouring was dusky olive, her features sharp. It depended on the light. Inside, she could look pale and wistful if she happened to be sitting alone, while outside, you noticed shoulder muscles, sturdy thighs and a glint in her brown eyes. Her body was smooth, flexible and mobile. He was reminded of what a dancer had told him: the art of posture is to walk with the pit of your stomach, not your legs. She did this naturally. Her whole body moved as one. She was beautiful in a way he had not encountered. The women he had known were pleasant and agreeable, sometimes cheeky, but beauty was something he associated with distance, even disdain, immaculate and unapproachable. Her beauty was natural and healthy. There was something luscious about her, like a force of nature.

At a later session, she waved across the room and he moved over to sit with her. The speaker was discursive and she made elaborate notes. She liked to write things down, she told him during a break. She made lists, for and against. It helped her to make up her mind, which was "weak and wobbly". He said, in a careful, understated way, that she seemed decisive enough without the prompt of paper. She was actually a "deep pond" person, she told him, slow to surface. "But by the time I come up for air I know what I'm doing." When the session ended, they wandered around the Australian National University, talking about spirituality. Her mother, who had died unexpectedly on a visit to the Banda islands, had been a Catholic. She had been at primary school when her mother died, and she remembered how the body had been returned for burial smelling of nutmeg. In her way of telling, the smell of nutmeg took on a sensual, and then a spiritual, quality. Her father, a teenage Indonesian freedom fighter and still a militant patriot, was a mystic.

She had been brought up by the family servant, Sumi, which accounted for many of her favourite sayings, such as, "The best place in the entire world is your own bed," and "A plate of rice never did anyone any harm," and "If you've got to wring a chicken's neck, do it quickly." She followed her father: she was *Kebatinan*, "You know, spirits in the stones and trees," waving away an inquiry he had not made. Each year she made a pilgrimage with her father to the graves of their ancestors. "At night we sleep in the graveyards." She watched the effect on him. "Otherwise I'm just a regular Sydney girl."

They walked together in a dark street on the way to a dinner party some friends were giving to celebrate her birthday. He wondered what birthday it was. "Would you like to come?" Unfortunately, he had another engagement. When they parted at the corner of a street called Darling, they kissed the edge of each other's lips lightly. A few days later she telephoned from Sydney. "Remember Darling Street?" He mumbled, covering his excitement. "Did you have a nice birthday party?" "Yes, except I was late. They were beginning to worry. You see, I met this man." She asked if next time he would like to have a meal with her. He said he would and they made arrangements to meet in Canberra.

They ate at Timmy's Kitchen in Manuka, so small and crowded that you conversed with your neighbours and even sometimes shared meals with them. He had king prawns, Szechuan-style, she had tofu hotpot. She was friends with the Chinese owners, who cooked, served and managed the till, which hardly ever stopped ringing, not because the turnover in the restaurant was quick but because of a thriving take-away service. As they ducked, sidestepped and swivelled around the room, they looked at her and smiled, as if she were part of their good fortune. She sat in the middle of the noise, alight with enjoyment, noticing everything. She laughed when something happened, like a popped cork or a dropped plate. For the first time, she ate the heads of his prawns. From that time, whenever they were in Canberra, they ordered the same meals at Timmy's; he discarded the prawn heads, which she meticulously dissected, and he ate some of the ingredients in her hotpot, especially bamboo shoots and tiny broccoli.

2

MARK WAS KNOWN IN THE Chandler family as the "money monk", combining celibacy (presumed, with familial innocence, in the absence of marriage) and devotion to wealth (assumed from the evidence of its accumulation). It troubled the family that he was still single. A man who was not married when he reached his late thirties or early forties was either singularly unattractive, unusually selfish, fatally unlucky, or even, perhaps, lacking in manliness. Not prepared to allow any of these judgments to settle on their Mark, they persisted in greeting him at family gatherings with questions like "Anything on the horizon?" or "Anyone in the firing line?"

He took it in good spirits. He was driven, he explained, by the need to make a success of the family business and did not have the time to develop personal relationships. He had qualified as a lawyer, he pointed out, but did not have time to practise law, either. Moreover, while not contesting the wisdom of the ages, he claimed not to feel deprived in his solitary state. One of the benefits of solitude was time and freedom to follow interests of your own, like poetry.

He had been so busy making money that it surprised people when he quoted poetry. The secret was not that he read a lot of poetry, but that he made good use of what he read. He never wasted a moment, keeping paper and pencil by his bedside to record something he was reading or a thought that took flight in the middle of the night, carrying pads or cards in his pockets, on which he jotted down points and quotes for speeches he might make. He had memorised Gerard Manley Hopkins' "The Windhover" and he would recite bits of it when asked. When he got to "level, underneath him, steady air", he would position his body and then, with "off, off, forth on swing, as a skate's heel sweeps smooth on a bow bend", he would veer away, swerving around the room with outstretched arms.

"Also," he said, defending solitude, "you can break wind in bed."

As a polished product of the Chandler family, he sometimes startled onlookers with pungent comments on the human condition. He had inherited his mother's charm and his father's looks, but also a strain of robust humour from his grandfather, who had been a pioneer farmer in the Mallee district of Victoria. The elements were not yet reconciled. "It's my upbringing," he apologised. "The animal physicality of country life."

As he became established in the world of money, women presented themselves with social invitations. He responded courteously, explaining that he was about to leave for a journey interstate or abroad, neither of which was necessarily true but, as he did travel a lot, not entirely untrue, either. He managed to sustain an almost intimate relationship with a sporty young woman he had known since school days. He kept on his desk a photograph of them together in Tasmania, which being an island had a reputation for secret assignations. Going to Tasmania as a couple meant only one thing, especially for those who had not been there, which was that you were "an item", without, as was typical of the alternative culture it attracted, any of the responsibilities that a formal engagement would have brought. However, in this case the excursion led nowhere. Tired of waiting, she married a celebrated footballer.

A young widow, whose husband had been killed in Vietnam, met Mark at a Mt Eliza Sunday party. She was mentioned in the family with hushed voices: a war widow engendered respect and sparked speculation. She had married young, faced tragedy and was still desirable, as well as mature and sophisticated. She led him into high-ranking circles in the armed services, formal dinner parties, and to her mother, also a war widow, and her sister, who was married to a naval officer. For a while, under the spell of women devoted to male heroism, Mark was tantalised by life in the armed forces. Men and women lived in the shadow of an arbitrary and insatiable authority that at any moment might require them to do extraordinary things, perhaps with terrible consequences, so they lived at a high level of attachment to each other and to the virtues of the civilisation they were asked to defend. He was drawn to the widow and her gallant family and friends, but she suddenly decided to live abroad.

When he asked himself to be truthful (awake, in the middle of the night, or watching a full moon rise over the silhouette of a modern city), Mark Chandler had to accept that it was not just his business interests that got in the way of marriage. He was looking for something that none of the women he met seemed to have. They presented themselves as competent managers of home and family, useful allies in the social world in which they expected to operate, companions on life's journey. They were faultlessly friendly, cheerful, healthy, always on time and looking their best, ready for whatever challenge was likely, but lacking an ingredient that made them irresistible. He wondered what it was. He thought he glimpsed it sometimes, passing a woman on the street with bold and steady eyes, but what was it?

The more successful he became, the more successful he wanted to be. This was not because of his nature, he submitted, but because of the nature of business. Business was not like the professions, where the rules of behaviour were clear, demand for your services constant and advertising frowned upon. Business was hazardous; your associates were rivals, not colleagues. It might once have been the case that some businesses seemed essential, and a long, even eternal, life for them could be predicted, but now nothing was certain.

Gold, for example. He had been brought up to believe that, whatever else happened, gold would retain its value, because the currencies of the world had to be pegged to something or governments would just print money as it pleased them. It followed that any business associated with the mining of gold, the commerce of gold and the manufacture of products in which gold was a component would never fail, because it was "as good as gold". Moreover, somewhere in the mist of national memory was the belief that the discovery of gold, first in the east and then in the west, had made Australia a nation, sealed in a tournament of physical manhood at Gallipoli. But his investments in gold had been a failure. The governments of the world, propelled by the same reasoning that had made the gold standard seem rational, deserted it and sold off their hoardings. Mark followed up his losses in the expectation that the value of the precious yellow metal must inevitably appreciate; it did not, and he continued to follow it down, until the stock market went into a flutter and the value of gold went up again.

Or speculation. Somewhere in Chandler family wisdom was a sanction against speculation, which was risky and had in addition a hint of sleaziness, even of illegality, because speculators, being forced to work for quick results, cut corners. A house built "on spec" had an artificial personality because no one had supervised the builder, who had undoubtedly used cheap material, covered with a slapdash technique. Also, the house had been constructed with an abstract market in mind, not a real person, and was therefore not "authentic". Yet Mark quickly discovered that to accumulate capital, you had to speculate, which he did, doing his best to pick winners among the stocks and shares. It was alright, he argued, provided you could afford to lose. It was like gambling. The danger came when you *had* to win to survive.

Among his speculations was a small exploration company. After an announcement of high quality nickel finds on one of its leases, the company's shares rose in value from forty cents to more than four dollars within a week. When independent verification of the quality of the assays was sought, trading in the company's shares was suspended, during which it was discovered that the material for the assays had been stolen from the deposits of another mining company. The chief executive resigned and was later gaoled, and the shares dropped below their original value, but Mark had sold substantially at the four dollar mark before trading was suspended and made what the newspapers described as a killing. It looked like a case of insider trading, but he said it was simply prudence. He had no knowledge of the stolen assays, but realised immediately that the value of the shares was ridiculously high. He intended to buy back at a sensible price later. People were making lots of money by buying and selling shares in the mineral boom and his good fortune didn't turn him into a celebrity overnight. But he was noticed for the first time. Before that he was just another businessman trying to make a go of it, up against the big companies and old money. Now he began to look like a winner.

He concentrated his attention on a family company that had a virtual monopoly of the luxury used car business in South Australia. He quietly built up a stake in the company, which was socially well connected in Adelaide's tight elite and well managed, and was invited to join the board. He then emerged as the cuckoo in the nest, secretly building up his shareholding until he struck, with a successful takeover bid that gave him control of the company, which he then sold at a handsome personal profit to a rival company.

Then he met Rukmini and everything changed.

3

When the bus crunched to a stop at the hotel where she would be staying, he trembled. It was a long time since his last relationship. He had become used to avoiding sex, or paying for it. She would travel to Canberra by bus, she said on the telephone, because she did not want to drive from Sydney alone. She made driving alone from Sydney sound like a journey into the unknown, an adventure in the Australian outback. She stepped down and took his hand eagerly, as if she were returning to him from a long separation. He helped carry her baggage to her room. She went to the bathroom, returning so quickly he wondered why she had gone there, drew the curtains, turned to him in the middle of the room with level eyes, calm and welcoming. She gave a small, deprecating smile, as if she had reached a point of no return, and then stepped forward and took him in her arms.

With one hand she began to undress, turning momentarily to fling away a piece of clothing. "You're very formal," she said, flicking at his clothed and upright body with the back of her hand. By the time he began to undress, she lay naked on her back on a quilt with a décor of squares, cubes and circles. Her body was more voluptuous than he had supposed from its formal outline. She wriggled quickly into a comfortable position and held up her arms, like a swimmer preparing to dive.

They later drifted into sleep in each other's arms. When he woke she was dressed, as primly as when she had stepped from the bus, a blue serge business suit, a cream blouse flecked with olive green, grey stockings, half-heeled shoes of black calf with a small gold buckle. She had made herself coffee and was reading a newspaper. "Only yours," she said, without looking up. "No one else's." "What?" he asked hazily. "Your slut," she said abruptly. "Oh, that," he said, with an embarrassed laugh, as if she had paid him a compliment. She gave him an appraising glance and resumed her reading.

This light prelude to their relationship became known as *The Bus Ride to Canberra*. The simple mention of it, like the title of a film, a book, a song or a painting, triggered an avalanche of smiles and laughs and half-finished sentences and shrugs and half-accusatory rejoinders, after which they would sometimes lock themselves in an embrace, hugging each other "for dear life", as she would say.

"God, what did you think of me?" A lopsided grin would give way to her brilliant smile. "But it worked, didn't it?" She reflected. "I knew, when I got on that bus, what would happen. I knew you would not take the initiative yourself, because you are so responsible about everything."

"I thought we were in for a long night on spirituality," he said.

"You did not! You *knew*!"

"I didn't, honestly. I'd never encountered anyone like you before."

"Oh, yes." She preened, doubtful.

"I didn't know what to expect. I'd been reading up on *Kebatinan*."

She had a habit of crumpling her face in disbelief, which she did now. "You're a knock-out."

"It crossed my mind that you might be an Indonesian spy."

"Oh, my God!" She faced him with hands on hips and a look of intense disbelief, which she achieved by opening her eyes wide. "Oh, my God!" She repeated the phrase as if she had just discovered it. "An Indonesian spy!" She made his suggestion sound as if he knew nothing about her opinion of Indonesian spies, or of spying in general, both of which were true.

He felt obliged to defend himself. "It's not unknown for intelligence agencies to recruit seductive women to do their dirty work. The KGB is staffed with buxom blondes. Mossad has its sirens. Why not Indonesia? Remember Mata Hari."

"She wasn't Indonesian, she was Dutch, and she spied for both sides, depending on which army officers paid her more for sex."

"Alright, not a good example."

"Seductive?" She assessed herself demurely and moved on. "Anyway, if it crossed your mind that I might be a spy, why didn't you stiffen your upper lip and leave me alone and frustrated in my hotel room?"

At times like this, he would look at her steadily, her lively face, now flushed, her nose with its sudden upward turn, her black hair swept up from her neck, framed in an open shirt collar, sleeves rolled up to dimpled elbows, gold-ringed fingers on low-slung hips, sturdy, smooth legs balancing on slender toes, and he could think of no possible answer that would explain why he went to her as naturally as if she were offering him something to eat. That she was irresistible? That she was so open in her invitation that it would have been ungentlemanly to refuse? He tried these and she laughed them away.

"If you had thought seriously that I might have been a spy, would you have done it? That's the issue. Don't try to wriggle out with ones, twos and threes from your logical mind."

His tenacity in argument was that when the manoeuvring ceased and the ultimate question still needed to be answered, or even asked, he tried to be truthful.

"The answer is no. I wouldn't have."

"There you are."

"Where am I?"

She seemed to be considering her position. Was she offended by the qualification of his ardour?

"You must have decided I wasn't a spy."

"Yes."

"Why?"

The first time they had this conversation they were in the kitchen of her little house in Sydney. She was wearing an apron of pink and green stripes with a chequered hold-all. The afternoon sun was streaming through a window, which needed cleaning. She was confronting him, wagging a wooden spoon, certain that she had the better of the argument. He grinned happily at her, because the answer had come to him.

"Because you came by bus."

Her eyes flashed as she returned to her stove. "You're so clever."

4

WHEN HER MOTHER DIED, MONEY from a family trust had passed to Rukmini, her sister and brother. She used it as down payment on a worker's cottage in Coogee in Sydney's eastern suburbs, which she turned into what Mark called a "stately pleasure dome", as decreed by the poet Samuel Taylor Coleridge in "Kubla Khan".

The little house was small and vulnerable, yet it had lasted. In its modest way, it had looked after families, weathered storms, withstood humidity, heat and the unrelenting glare of the sun, seen off the surrounding blocks of flats that had been built and razed, rebuilt and refurbished. Now, required to accommodate two lovers who were also busy, it turned itself into a workhouse, a storeroom, a fast-food kitchen, a seaside weekender and a pleasure dome, all in one.

It stood out in a street of nondescript charm, a yellow temple, more delicate than stately, rising above the roofs of terracotta, bonded beige and rusted iron. A small front yard beyond a picket fence was, when she bought the house, a tangle of pots, overgrown grass and the scattering of what had been a stone garden. On either side of the path were a ragged palm and a gnarled eucalypt, from one bough of which hung a cluster of bamboo pipes that rang like bells when moved by breezes from the sea but was protected from the harsh inland winds. Mark would later reconstruct the front yard under her direction into a calm space in which she planted lavender and roses.

Under the bullnose front verandah, the posts of which were painted blue, was an old rocking chair, the only piece of furniture that had come with the house. It remained, and a small table was placed at its side, giving it a presence and connecting it with life inside the house. A front door with leadlight borders led to a narrow corridor, with a red runner carpet from Turkey and a long side table with claw legs from Thailand. Two adjoining rooms – a front office and a guest bedroom – were neat and practical, but she had built in ceiling-high bookshelves of pale wood in the front room, making it look wider and higher, more impressive, which was her intention for this was where she worked and received visitors.

The back of the house opened up into a living, eating and kitchen space, with a strong sense of wood – bare floorboards, wall cupboards, chairs and dining table, even in the bathroom where the toilet seat was brown wood. Down a sharp flight of stairs from the kitchen was what she called "under the house". The slope of the land left enough headroom for what became storage space, cemented and bricked in, and a kind of all-purpose room, with a shower, opening onto a small garden and garage, which itself opened onto a back lane. Mark spent many hours in this part of the house, packing and unpacking, as she used her house as a transhipment centre for medical goods sent to Indonesia in support of student protesters, rough-handled by police and security forces whenever they demonstrated, and whom she called "freedom fighters".

But it was up the stairs to the second floor, where old gave way to new, that her sense of colour and form took over. The wood became lighter and the yellow of the walls stronger. The windows, draped in white curtains that billowed in persistent breezes from the sea, were angled to deflect the sun and to catch the shifting colours of the ocean. There were two bedrooms, a bathroom and living area containing two light blue sofas and a desk in a niche with a view of the sea (if you stood on tiptoe, which she would laughingly do). "The view is just for you," she said to Mark. She loved giving him things, and was embarrassed when he gave her presents, unless they were really extravagant, when she would chortle with pleasure.

In her bedroom, you wakened in the morning to the call of birds. Mark would descend the steep, narrow stairs carefully and make breakfast for himself while reading the newspapers. Then he would take up her breakfast on a tray. She had several kitchen trays, but he always chose one made of wood, with a raised edging that included cut-out handles. Her breakfast was always the same – muesli, fruit, reflecting her taste and the seasons (she loved mandarins and disliked bananas), a slice of toast or sometimes a croissant, brioche or muffin, and coffee. The breakfast tray always included a three-cup coffee pot with two brightly coloured mugs. He respected her need to wake up slowly and if she was not awake he would sit at the side of the king-size bed, waiting for the smell of coffee and his presence to disturb her. She would sit up abruptly, smile at him and reach for her first, long draught of coffee. Sometimes she would eat the toast, or its equivalent, sometimes not, in which case he would. Breakfast was his favourite meal of the day.

They would examine each other thoughtfully over their mugs of coffee, discuss the morning's news, reflect on what had happened the previous day or, perhaps, during the night. Sometimes, they showered together. He would then depart to his niche, while she worked in the downstairs front room. Mark stayed upstairs, leaving her to direct the human traffic downstairs, friends from school and university, people from the media and politics, the organisers of the gay and lesbian festival, which she enthusiastically supported, next-door and over-the-road neighbours, international travellers and visitors from Indonesia.

Occasionally someone would come to the staircase and shout, "Mark, do you want a cup of tea?" Or coffee. Or perhaps, "Do you want a cup of tea or coffee?" Or perhaps a piece of a cake or his favourite apple slice that had just been baked. They treated him as her appendage, but in a respectful, even affectionate, way, which he enjoyed. He was a successful man of business, grasping a few days of rest and recreation with his girlfriend. All his tensions subsided when he was in the house. She was in charge, a quick, light figure swishing from one room to another, looking over her shoulder as if she expected others to follow. He relaxed in her wake, as if the weight of the world had been lifted from his shoulders.

In the niche she had provided for him in the new upstairs, with its glimpse of the sea, sometimes inky blue, sometimes as green as grass, sometimes (in the afternoons) freckled with cloud shadows and sunspots or flecked with white breakers, he wrote up notes about political detainees in neighbouring countries. Through Rukmini he had met politicians from all political parties who were members of Amnesty International and he joined, the first commitment outside his business interests he had ever made. In the niche upstairs, he was doing his stint as an unpaid worker in the cause of political freedom. Still a pragmatic businessman, he had shifted ground on the nature of global order. He had also begun to think differently about Australia, seeing his country through Rukmini's eyes as a land of opportunity.

He would be working, lost in concentration, when he would sense her by his side. His hand would touch a thigh, a bent leg, a foot. Her lips would be warm on his neck. No words. She would leave him, return, leave, return, like a cat stalking her domain. Once, he had been unable to work unless he were alone, preferably behind a closed door, as if what was important to him had to be kept secret. Now all doors were always open and he was happiest when she was near.

Her bursts of enthusiasm, her instinctive judgments, her sense of drama with herself at the centre became part of the excitement of being with her. Their sexual life reached heights he had never experienced before; it was not simply an exercise in affection or pleasure but a reaching beyond themselves to something important. He was too careful and moderate a man to become passionate and intense himself, but he allowed her to set the pace. He had embarked on an uncharted journey, and he was surprised that he was not concerned.

Her favourite spot in Sydney was Watson's Bay. They sat on the grass, looking back through bays of curling water and tenanted headlands like jutting bows to the rise-and-shine of the city. She liked the seafaring atmosphere, the narrow streets, the rickety cottages seemingly kept upright by bougainvillea and morning glory, and she admonished the new inhabitants, glassy and steely with water views, with a dismissive wave of one hand.

They frequented Sydney's fish market, waking early, driving quickly with sleepy eyes to be in time for the freshest catch. She regarded herself as an expert on the selection of fish, which she always bought whole, chosen for the "look in the eye", buying enough for two or three meals, one more or less immediate and the others frozen.

"I once thought I would be a chef," she told Mark, before buying her favourite snapper. "That was after I thought I would be an airline hostess." She would grin at her foolish instability and, piling it on, would add, with one of those backward looks as she sped among the stalls, "I almost once went into computer software programming." He doggedly kept up with her, as you did with a child who was showing off.

They drove to where the Hawkesbury River comes down to the sea and standing on an outcrop of rock peered down the coastline, imagining that they could see the skyscrapers of Sydney, which you could on rare days when the air was unpolluted. In the Blue Mountains, they mingled hand-in-hand with the mist on rocky trails and afterwards ate heartily in rustic restaurants. Once, they stayed overnight in a cavernous guesthouse, billowed to bed in great waves of feathered quilts, when Rukmini woke in the middle of the night to exclaim that she was dreaming she was in the Garden of Eden. When she had quietened down, Mark asked gently, "Can you see the snake?" She cuddled herself self-consciously. "No, but there's lots of birds trying to peck me."

They swam in rock pools in Coogee and Bronte. One day, lolling up to their necks in a secluded spot, he told her of the rift in the Chandler family after the dismissal of the Whitlam government. The family was shocked when the Governor-General had sacked the Prime Minister, although his party still had a majority in the House of Representatives, but Mark was pleased that the economy had a chance to recover. The attack on tariffs, the oil price increases (not, admittedly, Whitlam's fault), rising inflation, the resignation of senior ministers and the intended borrowing of large sums of money from mysterious Arab sources had sent shock waves through the business community, which was relieved at the chance to vote Whitlam out.

Although for business reasons he did not proclaim it, he was, however, sympathetic to Labor, Mark told Rukmini, because it had more imagination than the conservatives. Being a conservative in a nation as young, promising and unfulfilled as Australia was like being a eunuch in a harem, he remarked, to her delight.

"I could never make love to a member of the Liberal party," she declared.

Roses everywhere, wherever she happened to be, his Melbourne apartment, her Sydney house. Replenished in vases, usually in the kitchen, or in pots outside, lined up to catch the sun, doused in cow manure, watered diligently. And incessantly encouraged. "I must go outside and talk to my babies."

They toured nurseries in the south-east of Australia on the lookout for a species that had caught her attention, visiting newly constructed French chateaus and Swiss chalets, old Australian homesteads, lost mountain cottages. He ventured to buy a Picasso rose for himself. It turned out to be a success, flowering brightly and numerously when the others were in recess. He then bought a sweet-smelling heliotrope de Gaulle, which could produce only one large flower.

She organised the tours. "I'm good at logistics." She scanned advertisements, flipped through magazines, telephoned persistently, checked with friends, looked at options, decided. He would be presented with the outcome. "We are booked in at ... on the Sunday night ..." His approach was to discuss beforehand what they wanted to do and then build the detail on what had been agreed. She didn't like that, because she could never match the complexity and detail of what he was thinking. "Let's just do it." She took over the organisation of their lives.

She toured supermarkets like a general inspecting troops; he wheeled trolleys in her wake. Every now and then she would throw him a smile or return from an unusually labyrinthine foray to unload her armful into the trolley and to touch him before departing. At the checkout she paid with one of her numerous credit cards, getting cash on EFTPOS. "You don't have to pay a transaction fee." Once in Melbourne, at the Prahran fruit and vegetable market, he was so moved by the sight of her weaving her way among the stalls, engaging the delighted stallholders in conversation, that when she reached him with her latest bundle of purchases, he took her in his arms and kissed her twice, to rounds of applause.

She cooked passionately, usually in large amounts. She believed that Indonesian students in Australia were not properly fed and she was always inviting groups of them for an Indonesian meal, especially to her Sydney house. In Melbourne, she also cooked in large quantities for him, he would find when she had left half-a-dozen meals in plastic containers in the freezer.

She became so much a part of his life that she was a presence when she was not there. He would think about her on aircraft, in offices, at conferences, walking by the lake to a meeting in Canberra. Once, driving alone to Lorne, he turned to an empty seat when, after Aireys Inlet, the long stretch of surf beach and the grey-purple, cloud-touched headland came into view. "Darling, look!"

They found they were spending more time than expected in Canberra, which was in any case a kind of halfway house between Sydney and Melbourne, so he rented a small flat in Kingston. She now drove her small car fearlessly from Sydney, stopping at Berrima for coffee in a shop where she established a kind of intimacy with the Dutch woman who owned it. "You'll see when you visit. She has the most extraordinary toes." He commuted by air from Melbourne. Whoever arrived first prepared a welcome for the other – if at night, turning on the lights, choosing the right music (happy, triumphant or merely inviting), placing a small gift on the carpet at the front door. They ignored Canberra's official panoply and its smart-casual fringe. Instead, they walked in moonlight around the lake, took sandwiches and a coffee flask at lunchtime into unkempt crevices of bush surrounding the new Parliament and walked on its roof of grass, raising their fists to democracy. They bought a bucket and trowel and scavenged on building sites for soil for their tiny garden. They drove to the top of Red Hill and surveyed the city, nestling in water and trees with the blue hills beyond. They lived for themselves, as they might have done in any city of the world. Canberra was their love nest, not the national capital.

They acquired things they wanted to share, such as a painting of an Australian mountain in a snowstorm. They visited the artist, a woman who lived in a small town an hour's drive away. Rukmini loved driving, although she treated all other drivers as predators. On country roads, she could not bear having another vehicle in front. "It blocks your view," she would say, passing. She would accelerate if a car approached from the rear. "Let them sit there," Mark would say. "You're doing the limit." But she would speed up. "They shouldn't do that. It's tailgating." When she was driving, she kept up a running commentary, as if she were producing the scenery. "Look at that. Stunning!"

"I love driving in the Australian country. It's so open, so expansive. When I am in Indonesia everything seems cramped. I feel free in Australia. In Indonesia I feel that I can't move, or breathe properly." When he was driving, she remained silent and often drifted off to sleep. He sometimes found he was talking to himself. When they stopped, she would immediately reveal what had been going on silently in her head.

"I will always be grateful to Australia for allowing me to develop personally. But it's been hard work. For years I sold things at the market."

"What kind of things?"

"Oh, oils. You know, exotic Asia." She rarely used the method of distancing herself from her words by quotation marks, indicated by two fingers raised on either side of the head. Rather, she left the words to stand on their own, while observing her listener with an almost imperceptible twist of derision on her lower lip. "And I sold perfume at David Jones."

She had almost become a beautician, after wondering about becoming an airline hostess. She had had roles in films. "Support," she quickly added. She had joined a gamelan orchestra. She was now teaching Indonesian language at a TAFE college and writing for a Jakarta magazine.

"Were you a good saleswoman?"

"Of course. What's the point otherwise? Some of the girls at DJs behaved as if they were for sale, not the product. They spent hours on their make-up. They walked about looking at themselves in the mirrors."

"I've never sold anything, myself." Mark spoke as if surprised to discover a neglected window of opportunity in a life so committed to business and its values.

"You're a top dog. Top dogs are buyers, not sellers."

"Well," said Mark, unwilling to accept her agenda entirely, "obviously when you're in business you're selling something, but I've never had to do it personally, face to face. That takes a special kind of talent." He spoke admiringly, and then moved to correct her. "In business, there's no such thing as a top dog. Not for long, anyway."

"Well, you're just gorgeous, so you don't have to bother about anything."

She liked to close off conversation with a flippant remark. She would reveal later what she had in mind. Now, she said, "Selling's for marginals, and we're good at it."

5

ONE DAY, DRIVING OUTSIDE CANBERRA, they parked at Lake George for afternoon tea. She poured from the silver metal flask she had brought, and produced two blueberry muffins. Mark proposed that they should mount a steep, wooded rise on the other side of the road to see what the view was like from the top. "Your walking shoes are in the boot."

She gazed in wonderment at the cliff face rearing up from the lake's calm surface. "It looks like a mountain."

"It's not a mountain. It's just a slope, a bit steep here and there, but easy to climb. Nothing to it."

She persisted in behaving as if she were being asked to abandon her sanity, and perhaps her life, but he was determined. He eased her feet into her walking shoes, took her by the hand and led her across the road. She followed him wonderingly. They ascended the first rise easily.

"What you do is stay on the ridges and if it gets especially steep, use saplings or bushes to pull yourself up."

Within twenty minutes, with only occasional screams of anguish, open-air clutches and support from his protective arm, they reached the top. A panoramic view unfolded and she ran from vantage point to vantage point with cries of delight. She was wearing long white woollen stockings and a red tartan skirt and she looked like a wood nymph.

"It's just ..." She hesitated before using her favourite word. "Stunning!"

The landscape was a palimpsest of green farms, brown land and smoky blue hills washed by the lake's grey waters, with roads like pencil marks from a child's hand. She twirled on a grassy patch. They linked arms and danced. Her eyes were like sparklers. When the time came to descend she strode confidently ahead.

"It will be easier going down," she announced.

But it was harder. The slope, which had been a steady incline when ascending, now seemed precipitous. She stood on a ridge looking down, scared and unable to move. Between the ridges were ravines, but their sides were also steep and the undergrowth below looked thick and uninviting.

"We have to stay on the ridges."

"I'm scared."

He found a dead branch that he broke into a piece about twice the length of a walking stick.

"You hold on to one end and I'll take the other. You go first, just easing your way down. I'll make sure everything is secure at the other end. All you have to do is hold on."

"Do I face backwards or forwards?"

"A good question." He put himself in her position. "Which way gives you the best hold?" Observing her, trying. "Try backwards. Then you can hold on with both hands."

She slipped and slithered down, pulling him with her. He dug in his heels, clung to tree trunks and grasped at bushes with his free hand. She came to a stop against a fallen tree and he clambered down to join her.

"We're doing well. Not far to go."

She peered down. "We're not halfway."

"We're nearly halfway."

She searched his face for some indication of the difference. "It's steeper."

"If we trek to the side, which we can if we head up again and then branch off, the slope over there is more gradual."

"Up again?"

"Yes, darling. Up, then down, more gently."

She looked at him fiercely. "You know what I want to do?"

"No."

"I want to stand on this tree trunk and throw myself into space."

"If you do that you might just escape death, but you'll probably end up in hospital."

"There! I said it was dangerous, this mountain."

"Only if you try to throw yourself off it."

He was developing a brutal undertone in his steady, sensible responses.

"What if I just run down?"

"You'll break a leg, or perhaps your back." He relented. She looked so helpless. "Look, just hang on. I'll pull you."

They climbed back to a spot where he had noticed a spine running off at a lower level, linking their ridge with another, the second one descending away from the direction of their parked car but on terraces they could manage more easily. He pulled her along, as if she were a prisoner.

"Come on. Nearly there."

She grunted laboriously over each step, as if it were an enormous achievement. She had reached the end of her physical, also psychological, tether, and began to cry. He came back and hugged her.

"Not long now."

She raised a tearful face. "I'll never climb a mountain again."

"Come on. Be strong. We'll soon be down and everything will be fine again."

"Why don't you go first?"

"You're not strong enough to hold me."

Grumbling, she took a deep breath, grasped the stick. "Alright, master."

This time, she leant her weight fully back, as if she no longer had responsibility for her fate, pulling him down at literally breakneck speed, but he held on as they rapidly completed the last stage and, eventually, in a series of staggers and jumps, they reached the road.

She trudged off, slow and unsteady on level ground, in the direction of the car. He followed silently. She did not change her shoes, although they were muddy, and sat quietly all the way home. That night, in the darkness:

"Darling?"

"Hmm."

"I'm sorry."

He put out a hand to touch her.

31

"If ever, in the future, I do something silly or you want to remind me that we are bound together until death, all you have to say is 'Remember Lake George!' "

"Remember Lake George!" he mumbled, drifting into sleep.

Remember Lake George! became, like *The Bus Ride to Canberra*, part of the language of their relationship, unknown to others, reminding them each time of its sense of self-discovery and evaluation. She uncovered later the lake's mystery, how it was believed by geologists to be the oldest lake in the world, how astrologers mapped its place in the stars, how there was more drowning and road accidents in its vicinity than in any comparable place in Australia and how engineers could not discover why its water level rose and fell so dramatically. She now spoke of Lake George as if their experience had added to its mystic property.

6

HE BEGAN TO FEEL THAT an experience was not fully understood unless it was shared with her. This extended to visiting art galleries, which he had managed to do alone successfully for years and in the course of which he had acquired some knowledge of market values but also of what people who had devoted their lives to appreciating art had decided were the qualities that would ensure that a painting would last. Now, whenever he was attracted to a painting, he wondered not what the critics had said about it but what she would make of it. She had no knowledge of what the scholars had said or what the critics currently thought and it never occurred to her that as part of a habit of visiting galleries she should find out, but she had garnered bits and pieces of biographical information and made her own quick judgment of the paintings.

She just walked in off the street and looked, as she might at a dress or a piece of furniture. Now, he walked in off the street with her and became engaged at once in her intimate, assertive, oracular judgments. He watched and listened, storing it away in his enchanted memory.

In front of a Monet: "He was tired. You can see, it doesn't have the feeling that it will last. This must have been when the family wasn't helping him as much as he wanted with his garden."

In front of a Nolan: "He doesn't understand the Australian outback. He sees it from the south, looking up. So it is forbidding, separating him from his European inspiration. But from the north, looking down, it is a welcoming space, freedom."

In front of a Picasso: "It is horrible. He makes the human body into parts, like a car factory. He has surgical binoculars, no inner eye."

In front of a Matisse: "His colours are so vibrant. He reaches out of the picture to you, as if he wants to make love to you. And his drapes and carpets. He must have loved those old hotels he painted in."

In front of a Renoir: "This must have been after he developed arthritis. He's not bothering about detail, just the broad sweep, with his poor hands. I don't myself care for Renoir, for some reason."

In front of a Cezanne: "Very composed. Mrs Cezanne looks as if she is getting tired of sitting for him. Or perhaps she is just getting tired of him."

He had for several years owned a painting by a woman that was noticed wherever it was hung in his Melbourne apartment, a swirling mass of blues in the centre of which was the nude figure of a woman, lambent limbs, alabaster skin, exotic features, with two prominent, rather hummocky, breasts, on one of which she suckled what looked like a squirrel but could be a possum or even, a horrified woman seeing it for the first time imagined, a rat. Women would stand in front of the painting, wordless, involved against their will. When they withdrew, it would be sometimes with a dismissive laugh, sometimes with a dark look of anxiety. Some would want to discuss it with him, occasionally at great length. He removed it to his bedroom, where only Rukmini and the cleaning lady, who long ago had registered her disapproval of the painting by refusing to dust it, were likely to see it.

She observed it calmly. Then one night, in bed, she asked: "Why did you buy that painting?" Struggling to recall the circumstances, he stalled. "It's a long story." "Not too long, I'm sleepy." "Do you like it?" "I've reached an understanding with her." "An understanding?" "Oh, yes. I talk to her all the time." "What does she say?" "She's in a strange land. But unlike that fierce woman in medieval armour you have on the stairs, this one accepts her new land, nurtures it."

"Yes," he said. "That's why I bought it."

She noticed his smugness. "Clever," she said, rolling over.

She said "clever" when she wanted him to know that he had failed to convince her. She regarded cleverness as an underhand way of winning an argument. Then she would resort to action. "Well, I'm not!" She threw off the bedclothes and pounced, astride him, laughing, bouncing, defiant. "Don't you dare try to stop me."

Her favourite film classic was *Les Enfants du Paradis*, which she saw at a film festival and ever afterwards badgered him to find a distributor who would screen it for their benefit. He succeeded eventually and they sat through it again, almost alone. She loved the hustle-bustle of the Paris streets, the hurdy-gurdy of the theatre, the make-believe emotions, the stilted dialogue, the rapid switching from comedy to farce to tragedy. She identified with Arletty.

"Her lips are always smiling but her eyes are always sad."

Another favourite was *The Sheltering Sky*, Bertolucci's film version of the Paul Bowles story, in which, after her partner dies on an epic journey in Morocco, a young American woman becomes part of a camel train and the lover of its leader.

"For her, it's not the camels and the sex, nor the social and political claims of Islam," she said. "It's a spiritual journey. She discovers her soul."

In cinemas, she would close her eyes and cover her head when the drama became violent. She saw her first opera in Melbourne. She sat upright and wide-eyed, transfixed by the drama and the music. At home, after the opera, they lay on the big couch together, hand-in-hand, watching the shadow of trees playing on the ceiling.

"The human voice is the most beautiful sound in the world," she said. "And the saddest."

"Why is it sad?"

"Because beauty cannot last."

"You mean it fades, like a flower?"

"Yes. Although it can last in memory."

"Well, then?"

She turned quickly and snuggled herself into his arms. She had a habit of throwing one leg over whatever part of his lower body would accept it.

"Life is big and relentless," she said. "It cannot stop to care about something as fragile as beauty."

When she was thoughtful, she sometimes walked around, aimlessly doing things. Now, lying against him, he could feel her limbs involuntarily moving.

"What about us? Won't we last?"

He had turned off the light earlier and in the silent darkness he could feel her warm body. One finger was touching his lips. The surface smells of her flesh rose to him through lingering perfume and cream.

"Of course we will." He held her tighter.

"Why should we be different?"

"Because we're not into beauty, we're into flesh."

Her finger pressed on his lips and entered his mouth. "Doesn't flesh wither and die, too?"

"The great thing about flesh," he said, as if he had just read an article about it in a medical journal, "is that it can be regenerated."

"You mean the resurrection?"

"No, I mean that the flesh renews itself naturally. Not the resurrection. The re-erection." His suppressed laughter brought on a bout of hiccups.

She lay silent for a long time, before pronouncing. "You're sinful."

She carried with her a card of the zodiac signs, of which he was mildly scornful. He behaved, however, as his sign Aries directed. Life was a serious business and he had the energy and assurance to deal with it. He was competitive, with the will to win. But he also had a playful side; if you wished to remain in control, and not let life's tentacles take hold, it was prudent to keep a certain distance. He did this with irony. He sometimes said his philosophy was "conscientious frivolity". She was a Sagittarius, which made her an Arian's natural partner, restless and innovative, but she had strong impulses of activism and discontent. She did not like her sign. She had detected a tendency to write off Sagittarians as flighty. She did not like the idea of being "mutable" or "versatile". Still, she liked her herbs, especially lemon balm, and pink flowers, she enjoyed her assigned stance, feet wide apart, hands on hips, and she preferred Jupiter to Mars. She loved diamonds, the Arian gem. She reminded Mark that she used only one perfume, Chanel No.5.

"Coco Chanel collaborated with the Germans," he said.

Her eyes smouldered. "Don't put me down."

He tried to explain that he wasn't "putting her down". He felt sometimes that she skated on the surface, unaware of the water under the ice. "You're a blithe spirit." He didn't say that was why he loved her. She knew that.

"I won't change," she said. "It keeps me young."

Her favourite poem was Judith Wright's "Woman to Man". She liked him to read to her before sleeping.

The eyeless labourer in the night,
the selfless, shapeless seed I hold,
builds for its resurrection day –
silent and swift and deep from sight
foresees the unimagined light.

She would lie quietly on her back staring with eyes wide open at the ceiling as he read. Then she would turn herself to him, snuggling under his chin until he finished the poem.

This is the maker and the made;
this is the question and reply;
the blind head butting at the dark,
the blaze of light along the blade.
Oh hold me, for I am afraid.

He liked to recite from T.S. Eliot's "La Figlia Che Piange".

Stand on the highest pavement of the stair –
Lean on a garden urn –
Weave, weave the sunlight in your hair –
Clasp your flowers to you with a pained surprise –
Fling them to the ground and turn
With a fugitive resentment in your eyes ...

She thought Eliot was too "wistful" and she found his "cogitations" too abstract. However, she agreed the poem had lyrical moments. "I like 'fugitive resentment' in her eyes."

Her language was a mixture of delicately nuanced Javanese and streetwise Aussie slang, which led to outbreaks of sudden crudity, like a sweet-faced child suddenly using bad language. Conservative in her dress, modest in her public demeanour, she never failed to shock him because it was so unexpected.

Once, she suddenly asked, "Are you a leg man or a tit man?"

"You're really something," he chastised her, a slow smile establishing itself somewhere between wonderment and disbelief.

"Yes," she said evenly, "but which do you like best?"

"Better." He could be pedantic when he was in the mood.

"Yes, better. Which?"

"If they're yours, I love them indiscriminately." He kissed every plateau and recess, every rounded form and knuckle, from her forehead to the soles of her feet. And when it was over and she was a giggling bundle of affection, she still gasped: "Yes, but which?"

But it was the intensity of her love that changed his life. Nothing else mattered when he was with her. It did not matter if they ran out of petrol on some lonely road in the middle of the night. They would be together. That was all that mattered.

She told him that their love was a spiritual journey that would never end, even after death. Her body was sacred to him; if she had to choose between death and betrayal (as they watched on television the rape-ridden ruins of a church in Africa), she would choose death. She told him that if he died before her, she wished to kiss his dead lips and wash his face with her tears, tend his body with flowers and oils for thirty-six hours before any other members of his family were admitted.

Astonished at first, even embarrassed, Mark learned to listen to her with a kind of wonder. In time, he began to accept her intensity as a way of living. Her bursts of enthusiasm, her instinctive judgments, her sense of drama with herself at the centre became part of the excitement of being with her. Their sexual life reached heights he had never experienced because it was not simply an exercise in pleasure but seemed to reach beyond themselves to something important, although he did not know what it was. "Welcome," she said, as if he had come home, and it sometimes felt like that. He always felt secure with her. He was relieved that she did not take drugs, and never had. As he grew older, he had a fear of being with a woman who was wild and uncontrollable from drugs.

He allowed her to set the pace and rhythm of their life together. He felt that with her he had embarked on an uncharted journey, and he was surprised to find he was not concerned. His formerly measured and balanced life was stretched and jolted, but he was invigorated, not distressed.

7

THEIR RELATIONSHIP WAS CHANGING. ENCHANTMENT had become commitment and commitment had created trust. By trusting each other, they learned from each other. His cagey manner, adopted in the world of business, began to soften, like a bud opening in a late spring breeze. She was a potpourri of intuitions and impulses; prodded and guided by him, she began to arrange them in some kind of order.

Conversation became a form of lovemaking, discovering recesses, touching tender spots. They spoke softly and listened carefully, facing moments of unexpected truth together. She developed a tactic to cope with his ability to analyse and remember.

"I wrote it down in my diary at the time."

"You could have been just as mistaken then as you are now."

"I wrote it in ink and put crosses in the margin to show it was important."

"Yes."

"Well."

"You could have been just as mistaken then as you are now."

"Well, alright, I'm mistaken, but it's not my memory. It's me!"

She was against abortion. Under no circumstances, even including the possibility of her own death or serious illness, would she agree to have a foetus removed.

"From the moment of conception, it's alive."

He spoke of the need for birth control, family planning, economic and social development in poor countries, but she waved him aside.

"I agree with birth control. That's not the issue. The issue is after conception – whether or not you kill another human being."

He persisted. When was a foetus a human being? Somewhere in its life, it developed the capacity to think for itself, so that if it were asked if it wanted to be aborted it would be capable of answering, presumably in the negative. "I leave it to the medical scientists to tell me when that moment has arrived, no easy task. When does a fertilised egg become an embryo? Has the egg moved up the tube and attached itself to the womb? When does an embryo become a foetus?"

Eyes wide open, she listened to him with mounting, occasionally feigned, astonishment. "Medical scientists," she sneered, conceding nothing.

He did not share her view of prostitution, either. She was opposed.

"The body is sacred. You have to live with it all your life. It should never be sold for money."

"Prostitutes provide a useful service. If it weren't for them, the place would be a testosterone battlefield."

She appealed to his better instincts. "These women are degrading themselves, just for your satisfaction or society's comfort or whatever you choose to call it. They will never be able to love someone fully and passionately after what they have done. You say they are providing a service to society, but society does not thank them for it. When their looks have gone they will be cast aside to fend for themselves in whatever way they can. Once a woman sells her body, it's downhill the rest of the way."

He would not be hijacked from utilitarian principles. "It's not just women. Some women are now earning enough money to spend on erotic extras, so there are male prostitutes. If you are lucky enough to find someone who is a lover in every sense, you do not need the services of prostitutes. But how many can say that? At some stage of their lives, they will be out of that kind of luck. You cannot make laws just for the lucky ones."

"I would never think of hiring a man!"

He told her of brothels he had visited. "Not much fun," was his summary. He mentioned kindly whores who washed you with antiseptic soap, pimply girls who sucked lollies and screwed up their faces with the effort, beautiful Asian women who would do whatever you asked of them.

"Why Asian? Are they different?"

"I suppose because they're foreigners and don't know their rights."

"They need the money, because they're sending it back to their families."

"Maybe. You never know. Are they doing it because of the money or because they think it's exciting?"

"You think they think it's exciting?" She screwed up her face in disbelief. "It's the money."

They agreed about loyalty. She believed in it above all else. "Once you have made a commitment, you stick by it." His view was complex, relating to identity. He accepted the need to live in the present, and even the future, rather than the past, and a certain ruthlessness was essential to survival. Without it, you were dependent on the mercy of strangers, which was dangerous. But he was repelled by opportunists who kept reinventing themselves.

"The knack is knowing who you are."

"That's why I go to the graveyards. After, I feel I can take on the world."

She told him of an affair she had had in Indonesia several years before of which she was ashamed. He was a person of authority in the government. She was placed under his supervision for training. She went with him during the eight weeks training period regularly, a couple of times a week, to a sleazy hotel in the port of Jakarta, Tanjung Priok. She had no feeling for him, she said, but he wanted her and she did not know how, in the position she was in, to resist him.

Mark did not interrupt. She surveyed him through tears.

"I didn't know what to say to this man. He was so persistent. I felt sorry for him."

Mark remarked, almost absent-mindedly. "It's simple. You just say no."

"You don't understand. You're a man in another culture."

"Well, explain to me."

"I can't explain it, now, afterwards, here in another country. It happened. That's all."

"Then why are you ashamed?"

"I don't know!"

Her face was contorted with the conflict of crying and trying to speak.

"I despise myself. And I know you despise me, too."

She was sobbing now. He comforted her in a way that had become a habit, patting her head, kissing her nose, holding her tight. Later, when her body had ceased to shudder, she asked, "Have you ever done that? I mean, not prostitutes, but someone under your control."

"No."

She burst again into floods of tears and then drifted, between bouts of sobbing that sounded like muffled howls of despair, into sleep. In the early hours of the morning, she shook him awake.

"Darling, I'm so happy with you."

"Good."

"You're my lover, my soulmate, my best friend. And it's good that you've never done it with anyone like that. It shows that you're different. We're different."

And later that night:

"Darling."

"Hmm."

"Muslim men don't like you to be wet."

"Eh?"

"They don't like lovemaking. They like to force their way in, rough and harsh. Ugh!"

He sat up in bed.

"What's all this about?"

"I'm just thinking how lucky I am."

He wrapped it up as *The Seduction at Tanjung Priok* and it became a manageable memory, like *The Bus Ride to Canberra* and *Remember Lake George!* The idea of her with another man bothered him for days, however. It was not just that she had surrendered timidly what she proclaimed now was important to her, which prompted the thought that perhaps she had surrendered to him for the same reason. It was the actual sexual act performed with a person other than himself that turned his heart over. He saw her on a hotel bed, lying on her back, welcoming her boss with open arms, as she had welcomed him that first time in the Canberra hotel. He brushed the thought away. Who was he to judge? How could she be held responsible now for something that happened before they met? She had told him – that was all she could do.

Yet the thought – the image of her physically entwined with the body of another man, allowing him to touch her and penetrate her in the most intimate way that human beings know – would not be brushed aside. It kept coming back, like an itch you know will cease if you stop scratching but that you cannot leave alone. Why torture yourself? Why not just let it slip away into the past, and be forgotten. But he could not. He might as well have asked himself to forget his enchantment. They were two sides of the same coin.

8

SOMEWHERE IN MALE CHANDLER GENES was a yearning for a small, calm centre in the midst of all the rivalry and striving that was the way of the world. The house that would suit Mark's immediate needs and future requirements did not exist, taking into account his lifestyle, flitting from one place to another, and seemingly open-ended future. He was unattached, mobile and money was available; his options were seemingly endless. The Melbourne apartment, although large, was merely a resting place between engagements. So he built not the perfect house that would anticipate all requirements, but an adjunct to Melbourne, a wooded sanctuary overlooking the sea at Lorne, two hours' drive away.

She liked it instantly. He thought this might be because it had the cottage look of her Sydney house and that floral mix of Australian and global botanica that only fervent nationalists regarded as foreign – climbing roses, potted geraniums, pelargonium, hydrangeas, hyacinths, agapanthus, lavender, native trees and shrubs, especially wattle. Secretly, he hoped she would notice the stone wall he had had built by a local landscape gardener, who rode a horse to work along the beach and had a romantic spirit. Mark had not noticed a latent curve of the wall until the gardener-artist drew it to his attention, asking him to decide whether to let it go, or pull it back. Between the two options was a considerable slice of land. His decision to let it go had been the right one. It curved now in a graceful arc above the driveway, which was also not straight, moving in the opposite direction, creating a satisfying balance when your eye brought the two levels together.

She did notice. "Good lines," she said approvingly. "Like Matisse."

A relationship grew between the house and nature. The house itself had a settled look from the outside and a calm, cool feeling inside. The cedar had turned a ruddy dark colour, the wood of the beams, floorboards and architraves around the doors and windows was soft brown and the furniture and curtains were simple and subdued. The effect, with Japanese paper lanterns, was unobtrusive, a quiet and secure space. It might have seemed spartan were it not for the surrounding green of trees and shrubs and creepers that could be glimpsed from every window. Some manna gums were removed when the house was built but enough remained for their heads to droop and toss between the house and the sky. Wattle, lining the steep driveway, created a blaze of yellow in early winter and a spectrum of blue-green leaves for the rest of the year.

Mark surprised himself by taking up gardening, spreading horse and cow manure bought from roadside stalls so that the soil's tendency to clay, baked hard in summer and even in winter inhospitable to tender roots, was checked. Beyond the brown and green of the house and its surroundings, which was satisfying enough, was something else, something that had been integrated, too, he felt, by opening up a window in the greenery here and trimming back there: the dramatic blue, or turquoise, or pea-green, or sometimes, in early morning on a hot day, flushed orange, or in winter grey and leaden, presence of the eternal sea.

It could be seen, if not from every window, at least from three corners of the house, which was high enough to overhang the coast road and the rocky beach. You could see, through the gum trees and over the roofs of houses below, the surf breaking and spreading over the sand like the lace on the edge of one of his grandmother's quilts. People on the beach were mobile dots, with dogs like scurrying ants. Toy cars sped soundlessly on a road that, when empty, looked like a wriggling snake. You could see the heaving bulk of the sea, the grey line of the horizon and the sky above, sometimes pale and shimmering, sometimes bright and busy with fluffy white clouds, sometimes heavy and motionless with dark, thunderous intent, sometimes in the mornings pink and at sunset streaked with red warnings.

Crossing the Arafura Sea

One early winter morning he saw an astonishing sight: on his right, the white globe of a full moon setting through the trees and on his left, a golden sun rising from the sea. And because of the intense mini-climate of Lorne, caused by the headland blocking the prevailing south-westerly winds, as well as the flippant southern breezes that sprung up on a warm day in the afternoons, the air was steadily moist and rainbows were frequent, often straddling land and sea, one leg in the forested hills, the other in the mysterious depths of the ocean, like a magically implanted beam of post-modern architecture.

Rukmini loved to lie on a summer's day on one of the sofas in the living room and look up, not at the sea, but at the treetops, gently moving in a breeze and through which she could see clouds drifting across the sky. She dreamed she was living in a tree house. Light aircraft buzzed past just above the height of the house, hugging the coast, and slow ships trailed the horizon like ghosts. Lorne could also be wet and windswept when a south-easterly blew steadily, usually for a couple of days, so that the sky and the sea and the headland were flattened into a grey mass, the horizon and the coastline blurring into each other, the landmarks, like the pier and the radio mast and the old hotels and houses on the headland, obliterated by sweeping rain. After the storm, a swirling mist clung to ravines and crevices.

They stayed indoors on those days, reading in bed, listening to the wind whistling and the boughs creaking and cracking, dreaming of wrecked ships and swollen rivers, drifting into the main room from time to time to find something to eat or to stoke the fire with red gum cuts or to help in the preparation of meals that became more extravagant as the weather blew harder. These were also the days for lengthy contests of Scrabble and computer games. There was usually a break in the late afternoon, when for an hour the clouds in the west would part and the sun would break through, bathing the stricken town in a perversely effulgent light. They would gather on the wind-protected side of the house for afternoon tea, ignoring the leaves and the broken twigs scattered over the decking, breathing the wet, fresh, bark-laden air. Or sometimes they would pile in the car and drive to the centre of the town to inspect the damage, like scouts of the State Emergency Services.

Mark enjoyed gloomy weather because it confirmed his theory that nature and humankind must find a balance between their existential forces. When the south-easterly blew at Lorne, the only form of balance available to people was to retreat to the comfort of civilisation and let nature take its course.

He loved his house at Lorne almost as much as he loved making money, and was beginning to love Rukmini. It was another love nest, blocking out the world. Not being religious, he believed there was an explanation for everything. His relationship with Rukmini flowed so smoothly, satisfying each of them without any apparent effort, that he believed it had about it a whiff of the perfection that was reflected in the orderliness of nature, even with its outbursts of temper, and of the free market, even with its alarms and failures of confidence.

When he looked at the Lorne headland, he thought he had a glimpse of an Australian civilisation. There was the sea, of course, that he loved, and the boundless sky and the great inland reserve of tall trees, and the sight of surf curling through the branches of gum trees. The surf, no matter how violent or strong, was the sea at the end of its tether and the trees were the guardians of the earth, their roots deep and old, almost as old as the sea. On that headland had been constructed human habitation without (as yet) disturbing nature, indeed without as yet making much of an impression on it. Whether Lorne's headland would become part of a civilisation, with powerful resources and distinctive values, or whether it would simply remain a civilised way of living on the margin, depending on the resolution of forces elsewhere, remained to be seen, but his heart lifted whenever he rounded a certain bend on the Great Ocean Road, glimpsed the headland and began the winding climb, because he knew that all the contending forces in and around him would be in balance when he arrived.

He wondered about the people of this Australian civilisation, whatever it turned out to be. Lorne had once been the holiday resort of farmers and pastoralists, but it was now popular with migrants from southern Europe – Italians, Greeks and Turks – who responded to its collision of sea and land with fond memories of Mediterranean resorts. They had not yet become rich enough to seriously test the Lorne real estate market, but they came for weekend picnics, gathering at the barbecues provided on the stretch of beach between the pub and the pier. Asians, too, including turbanned male swimmers and women who walked the beach fully clothed. Aborigines were rare, but this coastal strip was where an escaped convict, William ???, had famously hid in caves for thirty years, protected by a local tribe.

When he was in one of his dreaming moods, turning the headland into another Eden, Rukmini was not only an enchanting and trusted companion, but part of an evolving Australia.

She shared his enthusiasm for Lorne, but was unaware of the cultural nuances. It was the air she liked. The Lorne headland jutted across the prevailing south-westerlies and southerlies, creating a sheltered climate of its own. The sea air and the tall eucalypts growing down to the water's edge combined to make a potent brew of ozone.

"My lungs need sea air. The gas heating in your apartment is bad for the skin."

She carried with her everywhere an assortment of facial lotions that, while a mere sample of the emporium of skin cleansers and toners and enrichers at home, occupied a small bag of its own that she took when travelling. But often in Lorne she did not bother to open it.

"You didn't have sea when you were growing up in Indonesia?"

"The air is moist there wherever you are. But I love the sea in Australia. It makes you think over the horizon."

She liked to sit on a green love seat with a high view over the roof of the house. From there you saw, through the slim upper boughs and swaying mop heads of gum leaves, the brilliant white surf and, beyond, the sharp line of the horizon, dividing dark green-blue sea from azure-blue sky. He took a photograph of her sitting there, her legs crossed gracefully at the knees, her eyes fixed out to sea, a look of lost rapture on her face.

When he first saw Rukmini, Mark had judged her frank and lively face and manner to signify a lust for life and the strength and confidence not to be downcast if life took one of its unhappy turns. He was right, but she was also at times thoughtful, subject to doubts and misgivings. Long before they met, she had been thinking about her responsibility as a woman to bear children. She first considered a secondary question, which was where to look for the father of her children, and decided that she didn't want to be part of an elite producing well-bred children, like racehorses or performing fleas. She would like children to be the natural consequence of loving someone. At one stage, she compromised to the extent of thinking that the father should be Chinese, because the Chinese were clever and notably hairless. For reasons that she did not fully understand, but were partly aesthetic, partly political, in the sense of being opposed to violence, she did not like hairy men. But eventually she adopted a neutral position on ethnicity and nationality, even religion. She then returned to the primary question. Should she have children?

She decided she should, not because she felt a physical need to be a mother, but because, next to your own birth, it was as basic an experience as you could have. And bringing up a child was basic, too. She thought one reason men filled their heads with ideas of power and glory was that they didn't spend enough time changing nappies. Bodily functions brought your thoughts quickly back to earth and, incidentally, made a nonsense of the body as the temple of sexual worship that fascinated all those aroused, or perhaps artificially stimulated, people in the advertising agencies. The detail of upbringing, the perpetual preparation of small human beings to meet life's challenges, the constant watchfulness, the intricate knowledge required, medical, emotional, psychological – in short, the vast selflessness of parenting – appealed to her.

She worried that without a child she would be preoccupied with positioning herself in Australian society, whether to be on the left or the right politically, or for that matter, the centre, which version of whose history to accept, whether high art should be preferred to popular culture. With a child, she was irrevocably committed to the continuation of human life. True, there was a need for balance between nature and nurture, between parenting and social engineering, between loving a child and releasing it into a world shaped by others. But without a child, life was a game. With a child, life was a commitment. It brought out the best in people. "It will bring out the best in me," she thought, "stop me wandering about, wasting time on anything that happens to take my fancy."

Rukmini was uneasy about her status in the relationship with Mark, but she was too embarrassed to raise the matter with him. He had once said, in a playful mood, that he believed in "free love".

Crossing the Arafura Sea

It was a charming mystery of his personality that radical thoughts lurked, half-formed, beneath a conventional manner. As a businessman, he was expected to be conservative, and in many respects he was, but he retained a permissive, even licentious, streak that broke out from time to time. Rukmini wondered whether it was a characteristic of Australia, as if liberty, transplanted from centuries of trial and error in the northern hemisphere, had been released to run wild in Australia, given new energy by the expansiveness of the country, like prickly pear, rabbits and the cane toad.

The issue of the legitimacy of children born outside marriage had been resolved in a typically practical way in Australia. The law recognised "de facto" as distinct from "de jure" relationships, so partners and companions became almost as common as spouses to describe people living together. The media, in its pursuit of celebrities, had turned illegitimate children into a new kind of accessory. Mark was unusual in the sense that, unlike many of the celebrities whose lifestyle often included drug-taking, promiscuity and, if they were female, clothes that were designed to expose the body, sometimes grotesquely, he was conventional in most things. Politics, economics, religion, culture, all these were free range as far as he was concerned, where the individual had a legitimate choice, but the freedom to exercise this choice was stronger, he believed, if you were a fully paid up member of society, able to vote, invest or save or spend, acceptable in a church (or synagogue, or even perhaps temple or mosque). A responsible citizen, in other words.

If you flouted society's norms too blatantly, your brand (he would express it in business terms) became suspect and if you persisted, you were shunned. The Australian public was quick to judge and slow to change its mind. You were branded – as a liar (in football) or a chucker (in cricket), a radical or a feminist, a womaniser or a poofter. So if you were interested in really important issues, like war or peace, or reforming society, so that the weak were not disinherited, or managing (let alone eradicating) racial and religious prejudice, you were in a stronger position if you were not discredited by a fatal flaw. In short, behave as normally as possible if you want to do abnormal things.

Rukmini thought that Mark's heart and head gave him different instructions. A businessman may have views, even strong views, about the values a society should cherish, but he had to deal with the way society was. He knew that people did not invest in a company because they wanted to help it get established, or because it had some historic or national significance that should be preserved, but because they thought it would be profitable. There were fine judgments to be made about short, medium and long term investments, about security and risk and what range of profit could be expected, but when all was said and done, they invested their money in order to get more money in return. So in business you had to deal with a human instinct that was not only basic, but base. If you took any other approach you were unlikely to last long in the world of commerce.

She wondered if Mark might also be conventional in a way that was common in Indonesia and not entirely uncommon in Australia, in that, having the means to keep a mistress, he would prefer to manage their relationship that way. The great advantage of this arrangement from the man's point of view was that the mistress had to remain attractive for the cash flow to continue.

She knew she was attractive to men, and that in Indonesia they would pay for her favours, to the extent of a house and servants, car and driver and a substantial living allowance. Even in Australia, the land of blokes and sheilas, there were rich men who kept women "on the side", perhaps in another city. She knew how to act the role of mistress, how to neither confirm nor deny, how to maintain the right degree of plausible uncertainty, and if a distraught wife had to be confronted, how to do it with coercive style. She had her own house, she worked for her living; she was not a kept woman. But she cringed at the role of mistress. For her, it was not tinged with mystery and romance but with hypocrisy and inferiority. Except in the most unlikely circumstances, a mistress could never have a primary role in society. She wanted to do more with her life than give support and pleasure to a man. Also, her political antenna told her that single mothers were a fashion that could easily fade, if the economy contracted or if public sentiment took a puritanical turn.

It came to a head on a visit to Melbourne. Unlike Sydney, where she drove her little white car everywhere, even to the next street for urgent supplies of bread or milk, Melbourne invited pedestrians, at least in the area around Mark's place. It was winter, and she found that walking in public gardens and tree-lined streets brought something satisfying to the surface of her emotions. She first noticed it in the older suburbs with established deciduous trees, when the discarded leaves were brown and yellow, matted on the wet asphalt, and the trunks and boughs were black skeletons with just a few leaves still hanging tenuously, as if they had been pinned there by a child. On a visit to the Heide Museum of Modern Art, a few kilometres out, she walked in the adjoining park down to the river, where there was a mix of oaks and elms, planted more than a hundred years before, with eucalypts and other Australian originals, and although the indigenous trees had not shed their leaves, the ground under them was muffled and soft with leaves from the oaks and elms that had blown their way, and she had the same sensation.

What was it about the dying fall of autumn that was so satisfying? In Australia it was different from the northern hemisphere, because the end of autumn and the beginning of winter was also when the wattle flowered in all its golden glory, so that it wasn't a melancholy or desolate feeling. It was a feeling rather of security and comfort, as if nature was providing a soft and manageable version of its harsher self, whether the brutal punishment of winter or the barbarous diversity of summer. In the tropics, without the drama of seasons, you did not have these feelings, nor strange, weather-induced impulses of energy and resolve.

When she returned to the warmth of the apartment, Mark knew that a decision was about to be announced. She did not close the door quietly, hang her coat in the cloakroom carefully so that you could barely hear the rattle of the hangers. She slammed the door shut, flung her coat at the nearest obstacle, perhaps the lacquered Chinese grandfather chair or the Moroccan table or the jarrah sofa with the navy blue cover, or even just the foot of the twisting, honey-coloured metal staircase, and then strode into the kitchen, shouting, "Who's for a G and T?" Mark claimed not to have enjoyed gin and tonic before he met Rukmini, but he became a happy addict, winter and summer, because of the frothy, tasty concoction she devised with liberal douses of sliced lime. If there was company, everyone would sit in a mutual admiration circle, Rukmini crossing her ankles with satisfaction.

"What is it?" he now asked, sipping drinks with her in the kitchen.

"I've been thinking," she said demurely, as if for her it was a rare experience. She seated herself in one of the white, plastic chairs around the white, plastic breakfast table, and crossed her ankles.

"Yes."

"I've been thinking about children."

"Yes." Mark always sounded impatient when he agreed, as if it were an unfortunate necessity.

"I mean ours."

"Are you expecting something, or, should I say, someone?"

"No. I am just trying to be responsible." She smiled thoughtfully. "For a change."

"Well, let me put an end to your anxiety." He looked directly into her eyes. "The answer is yes."

He had been expecting something like this for some time and had been carefully preparing his response, separating tactics from strategy, risk from opportunity, short from middle and long term, as if it were a business prospect.

She was a visitor from an alien world that the powerful West had exploited and now wished to control, or at least to educate in its own image. She was welcome in new multicultural Australia, but behind the welcoming face was watchful old Australia. When the balloon went up, when the chips were down, when the numbers were counted, whose side was she on? She needed the legal security of marriage to balance the uncertain Australian attitude to its non-European neighbours, especially Indonesia, the largest Muslim country in the world, with a politically powerful military – who could be confident that Australia and Indonesia would always be on good terms?

As for children, he accepted that part of his responsibility for their relationship was to meet her need. They had gone through the pros and cons many times – their different ages, countries, cultures. He was confident that she would take on the management of children with such energy and competence that he could leave it to her, responding when she asked but otherwise assuming they were in good hands. He had noticed young mothers at his favourite coffee shop, coffee in one hand, the other holding a mobile phone or (the phone wedged by a hunched shoulder) working a computer, one leg rocking the pram of a sleeping child. She could do all that. He couldn't.

"You agree!" She showed her delight, or surprise, by standing up, and he moved quickly, taking her in his arms. She managed to deposit her glass on the table but his spilled liberally. He buried his face in her hair. "I love you, silly girl."

His response, even if careful thought had been given to it, was genuine. He could not imagine life without her, or only with a deep sense of loss (no, not even then, he just could not imagine life without her). She had touched him, and everything around him, with a magic wand. His work, his life – wherever he looked he saw the effect of her presence.

When he had wondered about enchantment, he had tried to define it. He did not want now to define how he felt about Rukmini. He wanted to experience it. This was a measure of the distance he had travelled. Enchantment had turned into trust and trust had turned into love. And now love was asking to be formally acknowledged.

"I didn't think you would."

He showed his disappointment. "I'm surprised you're surprised."

"I just thought, why would he want to take on all the responsibilities of marriage and children?"

"The answer is simple. If we're to stay together, which is what I want, we need to marry and have children." He beamed at her.

"Because that's what I want?"

"You underestimate my ability to get what I want."

She looked puzzled. "You aren't worried about the cost of children?" She searched for something he once had said. "Like having a small business without any customers for the first twenty or so years."

He laughed. He had probably said something like that when he was expounding on the benefits of free love and the free market. "I don't propose to disclose the extent of our liquid assets before we are married, but let me assure you, we can comfortably manage a couple of unprofitable small businesses."

She adopted a teasing look. When she teased, she became defiant, as if she wanted to flush out hidden truths. "It's not just my body – you couldn't bear to let anyone else have it?"

He could not keep up the badinage. His eyes suddenly became moist. "No, it was my body that tipped the scales. I couldn't resist the idea of you tending it when I'm a free spirit, up in the clouds, looking on."

She opened her arms to him, as she might to a child who had fallen down and scraped a knee. "I can't bear to think about it."

This was one of those times that both of them were consciously recording. She was planning ahead. Many uncertainties were now behind her. The children would be Australian. They would be educated in private schools, but not Catholic. Her Catholic schooling in Australia had given her some rudimentary knowledge and the elementary equipment for acquiring more but the nuns were not up with the latest in science and technology. Australia was a Western outpost in South-East Asia and her children would need to take advantage of that. But they would also need to keep in touch with their Indonesian ancestors, so she would take them to the graveyards. She and Mark would need to work out money arrangements. They should establish a trust account for the children. She would upgrade her superannuation. Should she become an Australian citizen? No, she would prefer to remain an Indonesian citizen for a while, with permanent residence in Australia. The best of both worlds. But they should consider getting a house in Jakarta. Her father's block of land was big enough for another house. She puzzled about the kind of house that would be appropriate. It could be open at ground level in traditional Javanese fashion, with air-conditioned bedrooms upstairs.

He was relishing the prospect of them living together. He arrives in a taxi from the airport. She is at the door. She opens it with a wide swing, smiling. There is a smell of cooking, music is playing, there are flowers all over the entrance hall. Or he opens the door and there she is, laden with luggage and packages, exhausted and irritable from some journey but overjoyed to see him. He has images in his head of them in the garden, walking in the street, at the fruit and vegetable market, shopping, strolling at the edge of a lake. It is like a musical, colour and movement, with a clear storyline. And, at the end, there is a warm and loving bed.

But he could not resist putting it all in a form that satisfied his sense of the ways things were done in the real world.

"Let's do a deal. Three items. We marry. One to you. We have children. Two to you. We live in Melbourne. One to me."

"Done," she said, and they shook hands.

Part Two

9

THEY WERE MARRIED IN PRAGUE, in a simple ceremony in a spacious room in the old town hall, with chandeliers and spread carpets on a parquetry floor; even with translations, it took less than twenty minutes and cost only $50.

The bride and groom were fussed over by officials who were determined to show that, while the secular state might not have the grandeur of the great cathedrals with which medieval Prague had tried unsuccessfully to emulate Vienna, it had its own modest elegance. A piano was available and a pianist was found, who turned out to be the kind of Czech they had already met at the airport and the hotel, droll and friendly, with a cigarette in the corner of his mouth, who might have been from an American nightclub of an earlier era. The bride and groom slowly wound their way up the red carpeted stairway to the marriage hall to the tune of several hastily improvised melodies he had at his fingertips – "Alexander's Ragtime Band", "You Made Me Love You", "Puttin' on the Ritz", "Ain't We Got Fun", and, in a flourish of irony, "Let's Call the Whole Thing Off".

They had chosen Prague because it was neutral territory, lacking connections with either Indonesia or Australia, and they could dispense with guest lists and the social paraphernalia that weddings attract. But something about Prague itself appealed to them. They shared a feeling that the Czechs were trying to express in their struggle with the orthodoxy of power politics in their part of the world an appreciation of human values that they were themselves trying to express in their own relationship in their part of the world. They saw Prague as the capital of the human spirit, irreverent yet resolute in its resistance to dogma and doctrine, violence and prejudice. The names Beneš, Masaryk, Dubček and now Havel were more familiar to them than the names of other political leaders in central and eastern Europe, reflecting, not just in resistance to Soviet communism but also German fascism, the desire of the Czechs to keep their own identity. They admired the way the Czechs tried to remain true to themselves and they thought, in a burst of public spirit in which they detected no immodesty, that they would be showing support for the new Czech republic by getting married there.

It was a morning ceremony and light came through a scalloped window, bathing the gilt and dark wood of the chairs in a friendly glow, giving a polish to Rukmini's dress of yellow silk. It was really a gown, reaching her ankles, and Mark was suddenly aware that he was marrying a beautiful, elegant woman. He was dressed, as always, in a dark business suit and he felt suitably humble in the splendour of her presence. The registrar was a large and ungainly woman, self-conscious as overly tall women sometimes are, but graceful in the way she held herself, in her slow and sonorous articulation of the simple words, in the light of happiness in her eyes, and her enthusiasm, as if she were personally pleased to be presiding on this particular occasion (and would doubtless be just as pleased at the next). They exchanged names and addresses when it was over. They would keep in touch. "I would be more than ever happy to do so," she said, in her overly precise and courteous English.

By chance, they emerged from the ceremony on the hour, to be greeted by hundreds of tourists who were gathered in Old Town Square to watch Prague's most popular attraction, a 15th century clock that on the stroke of each hour performed a medieval charade. A cheer and a round of applause saluted them in their matrimonial state, apparent from a late decision by the piano player to sprinkle them with confetti. Their moment of fame was short. All faces turned upward as two windows above the clock face opened and a procession of bowing apostles shuffled past. A cock crowed and the hour struck. A parade of cheerful Christians perched themselves on either side of the clock, making way for the dark forces that the public mind of

Prague at that time regarded as threats to the health and happiness of the city. First, Death, with an hourglass, then, Vanity, admiring himself in a mirror, followed by the Jew, with his moneybags, and the Turk, bearded and turbanned.

They blended with the crowd to watch the charade. The forces of evil clanked their way across the face of the building, as threatening as a toy train, but Mark noticed a tremor on Rukmini's lower lip. "Come!" he whisked her away. "The dark ages." He read from a guide book. "1410. Erected by Masons." He laughed. "The gloomy Masons."

"They were so sure of themselves," she protested. "They knew it all, when the sun rose and set, why God was in his heaven, who was good and who was bad. It all fitted together. They were wrong. But then, they created this."

She looked around her in wonder. The town hall was actually a complex of buildings with a Gothic clock tower, which was different colours in different lights but essentially a mixture of blue and yellow stone with darker trimmings. No adjacent houses were the same colour. The house in which they had been married was apricot pink and the house next to it was champagne cream. She stood in Old Town Square, radiant in her wedding dress, and invited in everything, past, present and future, with outstretched arms.

They walked to Wenceslaus Square, where so many of the great events in Czech history had been celebrated, or actually happened, but she wished first to see Hradčany Castle, having been puzzled by a reference in the guidebook to what were called the First and Second Defenestrations. The Czechs, on their ascent to civilisation, had discovered a peculiarly local way of dealing with opponents, which was to throw them out of high windows. Rukmini wished now to check the height of the castle's windows. So they detoured to the river through narrow and winding streets of small churches and shops selling Bohemian glass until they reached the Charles Bridge and, rearing behind it, the castle. A glance satisfied her of the efficiency of the method that had disposed indiscriminately of Catholics and Protestants, Hussites and anti-Hussites.

Mark drew her attention to the case of Jan Masaryk, foreign minister before the communist coup, who, according to the official account, committed suicide by leaping from a window. "One might lean in the direction of a Third Defenestration," he observed drily. Rukmini was horrified. When was that? Oh, he thought, maybe 1948. She looked around desperately. Where was the window? History for her was now, with herself at the centre.

The famous square, besieged with traffic, had a commercial look. She was puzzled by the name Wenceslaus. From her Catholic schooldays, "good" King Wenceslaus had been a benign figure in a Christmas carol but the Czech accounts she now read made him a drunken tyrant with a vile temper. They were swept up on arrival by a horde of students, who walked fast as if they were intent on a destination at a particular time, but sang and chattered to each other as if they were on a spree. She accosted them with the guidebook and her question and discovered that like the Napoleons of France there were several Bohemian kings with the name Wenceslaus. The Saint and the Defenestrator were half a millennium apart. She sauntered down the square as if she had suddenly come to understand the Czech republic and its people.

"Let's buy a brick!" She was standing beside a tower of bricks four metres or so high. A young woman with an open face passed the bricks up to a wire-haired young man, who ingeniously placed them in a circle while remaining seated on his handiwork. Each brick (costing $5) would help to buy a house that would provide resources for teaching people with learning disabilities. They bought a brick. She wrote their names on it, with a heart in the middle.

Rukmini kept a journal of their short stay. She recorded her feelings, just as she recorded what she called the facts. As they took their vows to each other, she wrote, she was glad they had journeyed far to be married, glad that they had decided to make their marriage a special occasion, so that Prague would always be for them a symbol of something important. She noted that in their hotel that afternoon, in a flurry of cushions and pillows, they made love for the first time as a married couple. "There was something different," she wrote. "It must have been all that history. You suddenly realise how important it is to understand what you're doing, because that's the way it will be seen in the future. Everyone will assume that you knew what you were doing. Anyway, I wasn't as warm and creamy as usual. I didn't throw myself around the way I usually do. I lay straight and serious."

They embarked on an eccentric honeymoon, a few days in each of six different places, three chosen by each. She was delighted and embarrassed. "Won't it be expensive?" Mark put on his man-of-the-world face. "The Aussie dollar is holding up." She chose Giverny (for Monet's lily pond), Granada (for the Alhambra) and South Africa (because of the Dutch connection with Indonesia and she wanted to see how its Truth and Reconciliation Commission worked). He chose Moscow (because he had never been there), New York (because he had a business appointment) and Harvard College (he had booked them for a lecture series on "failed states").

In Moscow, their hotel had mysteriously lost their booking, although it had been confirmed, and all rooms were occupied. They were forced to take a hotel on the city's outskirts. They took walks to escape the drunken violence that surged through the corridors of the hotel day and night, the oppressive watchfulness of the foyer and the inertia of the dining room. They walked down dirt lanes through farms and cottages with ramshackle gardens.

"Look!"

A wooden house painted white with blue fretwork trimmings. A vegetable patch. A woman with a shawl across her shoulders weeding among the vegetables.

"That's the kind of house I would like."

"In Sydney?"

"Why not. Well, maybe the Blue Mountains."

"What do you like about it?"

"It's old and it hasn't changed."

"You're sentimental. They're hard to heat and cool."

"No, I'm loyal. To old things – and people."

The woman heard them and walked across, carrying a carrot. With a flash of gold teeth, she handed it to Rukmini. Her face beamed, her eyes were alight with a mix of curiosity and goodwill, while she gestured aimlessly.

"She wants us to eat it!"

"How can you tell?"

"What else can you do with a carrot?"

"It's a bit earthy."

Rukmini cleaned earth from the carrot with a couple of tissues, bit into it heartily, then gave it to Mark, who after wiping it on a sleeve matched her bite. The woman clapped with delight. She ran back to the vegetable patch, returning with a turnip.

"Look what you've let us in for."

"Vegetables are good for you. Especially after the glue we've been getting at the hotel."

Rukmini wiped the turnip and bit into it lovingly, passing it to him. He nibbled a dutiful portion. She thanked the woman profusely, knowing that nothing she said was understood. The woman watched her face in fascination, touched her cheek, stroked her neck.

"Indonesia," Mark said.

The woman blinked at him.

"Australia," he said, pointing at his chest.

The woman blinked on, disregarding the geographical shift. She looked into both their faces, one, then the other. She seemed to be searching for something. A memory, a person perhaps. Her eyes filled with tears. Then she turned, dropped her arms by her sides and plodded slowly back to the patch.

"Poor old thing. I wonder what she wanted."

They were silent until they came to a house of black wood tucked away among shrubs and trees, barely visible from the winding dirt road.

"I find this kind of place very difficult to walk past," Mark said.

"Difficult?"

"Whenever I see a place like this, I want to stop."

"Stop the world, I want to get off?"

"When we're driving in the Australian country and you're holding forth on how free you feel, I'm being pulled in another direction. I see a homestead tucked away in the trees and I want to stop the car, go to the house, knock on the door, meet the people living there ..."

"And stay there forever?"

"Yes." He was surprised that she might also feel like that and he examined her face for confirmation.

"When I feel like that," she said, "I just drive on. Faster."

"Well, so do I, if not faster. But the feeling has always been strong, even when I was a boy. And it has nothing to do with Australia. It can be anywhere."

Waiting in Paris for the train to Giverny she told him of an unhappy childhood, her parents early out of love, her father, in anger and unhappiness, creating physical havoc in the house, smashing crockery, sweeping cutlery from the dining table before stalking into the night, using his belt on the children, perpetually in some kind of liaison with the female servants. Her mother, frightened of him and insecure in a country that she had conscientiously adopted but was not her own, sought protection in her faith.

Rukmini said she had been raped by a servant when she was six. Mark glanced at her anxiously.

"Raped?"

"Well, yes, I suppose. I mean, I had no idea what he was doing. I was a lively, inquisitive child and I probably went along with it up to a point, but not that far. It hurt, for a start."

"What was his age?"

"Oh, fifteen or so."

"So, the idea of being raped was something you learned about later."

"The word, yes. But not the act. There was blood and my mother made a huge drama, I had to go to hospital for tests. I knew something terrible had happened, even if I didn't know what to call it."

"How did you feel about it? How do you feel about it now?"

"As a child, I wrapped it up in a parcel and put it somewhere out of sight. Hid it. For years I think I forgot about it. Then I had a *soiled goods* period. Women of mixed race in Indonesia are regarded as born whores. So I had more than the usual anxieties about acceptance. If a boy was interested in me, what was he interested in? Then, when I came to Australia for the end of high school and university, women's liberation was in full swing. In my ratbag feminist phase I dealt with it as you might expect – bloody men!"

"Now?"

She looked at him. Mostly, her eyes darted about, rarely in one place for long. Now she was looking at him steadily.

"Now, it doesn't seem to matter any more."

"You've forgotten?"

"No, I think about it a lot, actually. But with curiosity, not anxiety. There's so much horror in the world that my little episode hardly seems to matter."

He told her of a sportsmaster, handsome and popular, husband and father, who invited early teenage boys to his loving home in order to slip into bed with them ("Got room for a mate?"), fondle their pulsing penises until the inevitable relief occurred, and then, as a true gesture of equality, offer his own for similar treatment.

"I read about people who think they been have ruined for life by this kind of thing, but I have never felt that way. I went to sleep as soon as he left my bed. We had breakfast together the next morning as if we were the same people we had always been. Full of football chatter ... You've got to get that pass from the centre to the half-forward line under control. It's the key to the way the team works. If we can get it out of the centre like that, we're unstoppable ... And so on."

On the train to Giverny, she was as excited as a schoolgirl, her knees held tightly together, her shoulders twisting in spasms of delight and expectation, oblivious to the rolling countryside, with its copses, fields and meadows, single-span bridges over hidden streams. She was on the platform by the time he had gathered their few belongings. She stalked ahead, pointing extravagantly in the direction they were taking. He caught up with her in a one-way street, the other side sloping away to rural France.

"Hey!" His injunction made her hurry even faster. "I can't wait." He forced the pace, moving ahead of her. "I noticed."

"What are you looking at?" She knew he was looking at her, noting the high colour, the tossed-back hair held behind her ears, the profile tilted up as if she were searching the sky, the gold-ringed fingers swinging in marching mode. She tossed her head and hurried on.

When they arrived, entering near the studio barn, with the formal garden and the house to the right, she bought tickets, and then disappeared, after announcing, "I'll see you back here in half an hour." He wandered aimlessly, noting how the apple and pear trees were espaliered along a waist-high fence. He entered the house via a cumbersome kitchen, climbed with other tourists the narrow staircases, noticing a Japanese influence in a selection of prints, observed the genteel bedrooms, drifted down to the lily pond and the famous wooden bridge, overhung now with photographers, rested on a garden seat, missing her, wishing the time would pass more quickly.

She was waiting in the studio with a bundle of prints and calendars – the garden Monet saw from his studio at Vétheuil in 1880 (when he was 20), a mother and daughter in a field of red poppies, a woman with a blue sunshade in a brilliantly lit field of spring flowers and three poplars, women in a garden, their hooped and embroidered gowns of cream, peach and striped blue, a burst of purple and pink flowers from Giverny itself, women with parasols walking across a blue-sky landscape, an orange haystack in a white-yellow spring field. And the lily pond.

"I'm going to have a pond like that one day," she said.

On the plane to Granada, Mark read Washington Irving's *Tales of the Alhambra*, and they stayed in a hotel named after him. She read an account of noble families, the Zegris and the Abencerrages, whose feuds, she said, were responsible for the fall of the city, after a long siege, to the Christian Castilians (under Ferdinand and Isabella) in 1492 (the year Christopher Columbus discovered America, she noted, with a hint of pride at her discovery). Ferdinand and Isabella were buried near the Alhambra, but she would not visit the site. She regarded Isabella as a bigoted woman who treated Jews and Muslims like scum, revived the Spanish Inquisition and was responsible for the desecration of the Alhambra itself after the Moors were expelled from Spain. It was restored in the 19th century and had been maintained by Spanish authorities and private international support since.

The intricacy and delicacy of the architecture captivated Rukmini. The geometric designs, honeycomb vaulting, open courts and fountains were familiar, but the proportions seemed subtly different, less like a fortress, although technically it was one, and more like a redoubt, vulnerable. Was it just her imagination?

"They were a long way from home," she reflected.

"They were propelled there by the notion of holy war, which meant conquest," he reminded her.

They explored the palace of kings, the quarters of nobles and officials, the waiting rooms for emissaries, gardens, formal within the citadel, unruly and luxuriant outside, trellised, in plots and in huge pots. He measured the height of buildings with his eye, held out his thumb for perspective. They walked up and down through woods to the old city of Granada. At night, they made love in a room whose window was scraped by a sighing bough.

"There's something about that place," she said, when they were in a bus on the way to the airport. "It makes you believe in history again."

"How can you believe or not believe in history? It just is."

"You feel its presence there." She was delighted and intrigued. "Maybe it's because it's not just winners' history. The losers are there, too."

It was another of her effortless shafts, simple perceptions that explained everything, history, religion, politics. She kept returning to the grandeur of the period of the Alhambra, when religion and the state were one. The inhumanity was terrible, but there was something... about it. She could not find the right word, but persisted.

"Stunning?" It was her favourite word, so he used it ironically.

She turned on him with a glint in her eye. "You're mischief all over." She relented at the airport and bought him *Treasures of Islam*, published by the Musée d'Art et d'Histoire, Geneva. She inscribed it: "A warm heart and an open mind make a good travelling companion."

Mark's business engagement in New York was expanded at Rukmini's request to the Holocaust Museum in Washington. She stood transfixed before a huge pile of shoes. The smell of the museum stayed with her afterwards, not musty, because it was efficiently air-conditioned, but stale and lifeless, as if the story it had to tell needed a staging of things as dead as those who had once worn them.

"The only difference in Indonesia is they'd be sandals," she said to Mark, her eyes filling with tears. "If you made a pile like this, you'd start with the killings in 1965 and 1966 and go on, Aceh, West Irian, Timor, Lampung, Tanjung Priok, Petrus. The pattern is always the same. It has to be done for reasons of national security, or the wellbeing of the people, or to uphold the law and keep order. What law? The law in Indonesia is what the president at any given time says it is. The legal system is his creature. The pattern is always the same. A few dead are officially acknowledged, while the real numbers are ten or twenty times higher. Why? Because that is what the military is trained to do. The heads of those soldiers are filled with one simple order. Mow them down. But the higher-ups, those who have been to officer schools in the United States and Australia, know that what they're doing is illegal. So they pretend the numbers are low and say it was an unfortunate incident."

Mark listened in respectful silence as they moved towards the exit.

"They are killing their own people! They have been doing it for years. And they do it in the name of the Indonesian nation. It's just the same as the Nazis, except that the Indonesian military don't target one group, like the Jews. They'll kill anyone who disagrees with the government."

She turned to him in desperation. "They have to be told. 'Stop killing your own people. If it's law and order you want, use rubber bullets, shields, batons, tear gas, whatever you need, but stop the killing!' "

"It's not only in Indonesia." He was trying to ease her pain.

"Where's the killing in Australia? Everyone gets upset when a single person is winged by a policeman. Is Indonesia at a different level of civilisation? I won't accept that."

In bed that night, she suddenly asked, "So where is the flesh now?"

"What do you mean?"

"I mean, the Holocaust makes glorification of the flesh look silly. It's like a picture of a film star fifty years later – the shine, the bloom, the shape has all gone and there's nothing there. Just photographs and a pile of shoes, hair combs, gold teeth fillings, wedding rings and cufflinks."

She looked at him steadily, without feeling, yet with a startled expression, a manner she adopted when she found something hard to understand, as if she had to get rid of all emotion in order to concentrate on what was strange or important.

"You're not saying, are you," asked Mark, "that Hitler was trying to draw attention to the spiritual quality of life?"

"I'm not *saying* anything. I was only thinking aloud, asking myself."

He paused, allowing her an opening, which she did not take. "You sometimes understand things I don't. But if I pushed myself to *say* something, it would be the opposite of that. For Hitler, there were different kinds of flesh – Aryan flesh, which he glorified as representing the future of the German nation and the human race, and Jewish flesh, which was no better, worse, than meat in the butcher's shop."

She was silent, so he added, "The Holocaust illustrates the truth of a caption I read once under a Dürer engraving: 'We live by the spirit. The rest belongs to death.'"

"Why is it called the Holocaust?" she asked. "I mean, Pol Pot was worse, per head of population. And Stalin?"

"History. Hitler lost the war. No one who wants a public career, left or right in politics, even among the Germans, will take up the cudgels for him. Also, aesthetics. It wasn't just old-fashioned brutality like prisons and torture and forced labour. It was calculated and precise, using the latest technology, as meticulous as a Mercedes Benz, in a country that has made a great intellectual and artistic contribution to Western civilisation."

"I think it's also because the Jews have financial and cultural influence in the West," she said. "And, as far as I'm concerned, I'm glad they have. We need to remember."

She disliked Washington ("cold and insincere"), but she enjoyed Harvard. They drank red wine in the snow and watched the spilled liquid form pink streams that mingled.

"Like our lives," she said.

They sat through long and complex lectures together, as if their future depended on understanding what was being said. They ate in student cafés, part of the buzz of excited talk. On the bank of the river Charles, within sight of John F. Kennedy's inaugural address engraved in stone, they discussed politics. He thought Australia was different from the United States in an essential respect, which was that Australia could never expect to become a great power, dominant in its region. With Canada to its north, Mexico, Central and Latin America to its south, the United States was in the middle of an essentially Christian community. Australia had only the cold waters of the Antarctic to its south, while north were overwhelming populations, all the religions of the world and a diversity of cultures, politics and economic systems. Japan, China, India, Pakistan, Vietnam. Indonesia, the largest Muslim country in the world! The great test of Australian intelligence over the next century or so would be how to remain essentially Western in values while accepting other values and other historical experiences in its region as just as valid.

She listened politely, as if required to pay attention to a teacher without talent, and then made her own position clear. She thought the United States was a bully and the American people were arrogant. They thought they were not like other people, and that being exceptional entitled them to tell other people what to do, rather than suggesting that it might be wise to keep to themselves. She submitted a long list of hypocritical American actions she had compiled from listening to campus critics.

"Do as I say, not as I do."

"What about democracy?"

He knew she was unsure about democracy. She was concerned that fundamentalist Muslims wanted to take over in Indonesia. She agreed that if they tried to take over by coup d'état or revolution, the state was justified in suppressing them. But if they won a democratic election, what could be done to stop them unless a religious state was made illegal under the constitution? The dilemma for Indonesia was that the state needed the military to keep the Islamists from taking over, and a powerful military was a threat to democracy.

She used some new-found knowledge from the lectures. "The Americans don't have a patent on democracy. I'd rather have the English version. Or the Japanese. American democracy is harsh and unforgiving, and at the same time sentimental. To succeed, you have to become unfeeling, with a turtle skin, while inside you are slobbering, like a puppy dog."

"You'd prefer *noblesse oblige* democracy, a monarchical state keeping the lower orders in line?"

"Oh, well, then the French version."

"You mean, the cultural state. *L'état, c'est moi!*"

"I mean, not telling everyone all the time how great you are. You know I don't speak French."

An hour later, she suddenly said, "They're all so proud to be American, but you never feel they want to *settle down* in their own country. They all want happiness but they're never happy. What kind of a model for the rest of the world is that?"

It was at Harvard she invented the "one system, two countries" slogan. They had met a Chinese dissident who had been in the famous demonstration at Tiananmen Square and was now in exile. In the discussion afterwards, Beijing's pragmatic solution to the issue of Taiwan's status, one country, two systems, was mentioned.

"We are the opposite," she said, as they walked hand-in-hand across Harvard Square. "Two countries, one system. Indonesia and Australia."

"Sounds good, but is it true?"

"I don't know, but it's easier to say than your thingo."

Mark's vision of a secular, humanist, transparent, democratic world order was linguistically difficult for Rukmini. She agreed with its sentiment but as a defensive gesture had taken to referring to it sarcastically as "thingo".

In South Africa, they attended sessions of the Truth and Reconciliation Commission in Port Elizabeth. They visited the police station where Steve Bilko had died in custody. They walked along a grassy embankment overlooking a sports ground, where Australia's Test cricketers had played. They stayed at a bed-and-breakfast, with white-quilted beds and egg-and-bacon breakfasts and they felt like wayfarers.

She was excited by the idea of "truth and reconciliation". She liked its honesty: if your motive for the crime was political and you confessed, you were given amnesty. The decks were cleared, terrible wrongs were acknowledged, the relatives of those tortured and killed now knew what had happened and could grieve realistically, the state was exposed as torturer and murderer, which was a salutary reminder of what it could become in unscrupulous hands. In the judicial process, by contrast, guilt was more often than not denied, the truth rarely established, the state protected by claims of confidentiality and security, friends and family of victims often left in emotional limbo. And in time – a couple of years, a decade, half a century – the guilty become martyrs.

He tested her. Yes, truth was important and the adversarial legal process rarely uncovered it. But justice, he thought, was as important as truth, less profound perhaps but socially powerful. Truth might set you free (although, an essentially private man, he had doubts), but people wanted order as much as they wanted freedom, perhaps more. They did not associate order with truth, but they did associate it with justice. Punishing wrongdoers satisfied a public need for moral standards and orderly behaviour. It also met a human desire for revenge, not a virtue, true, but deeply felt.

Crossing the Arafura Sea

If Indonesia had a truth and reconciliation commission, would not the guilty stay on top because they had the money and the power to restore their reputation and the Indonesian people were not vindictive? The military, government ministers and senior bureaucrats, the president and his associates, business people – they didn't do the dirty work. They paid someone to do it. You would never be able to trace a command to any of the real culprits. The deeds were by underlings, the word was by mouth, the money was in cash, delivered in brown paper bags by couriers who half the time did not know what was in the bags or why they were delivering them. Obedience to authority and a reluctance to accept responsibility were such ingrained attributes that the truth and reconciliation process would not make a dent.

She listened in silence. He was probably right, but she did not like what he was saying. Indonesia was her country, not his, and she wanted something that would set her people free. She brushed aside his quibbles about truth and justice and liberty and order. What about poverty? So many people all around the world were poor, yet some countries, like the United States and Australia, had more than enough for their own people. In fact, Americans were consuming themselves to death. They were overweight and they drove everywhere in gas-guzzling cars, polluting the atmosphere.

Why was poverty allowed to continue? She stamped a foot and glared at him, hands on hips, as if he were deliberately concealing the answer. "What about Australia?" she demanded. "You could do with a bit of truth and reconciliation with the Aborigines."

On the flight from Johannesburg, they saw ice floes from the south on the dark blue waters of the Indian Ocean, and they held hands. She told him that whenever she thought of outback Australia, she was frightened of being hit by an asteroid. She had read in a magazine at a doctor's surgery that the exposed metal surface of the old Australian continent attracted asteroids. To his raised eyebrows, she retorted: "Well, there were pictures of the craters, all over the Australian outback. What's your explanation?"

He had none, but suggested it was pointless to be frightened by something you could do nothing to prevent.

"But that's why I'm frightened. If I could do something about it, I wouldn't be."

10

RUKMINI RENTED OUT THE YELLOW house in Sydney and moved to Melbourne. Immediately, she set about renovating Mark's apartment. Houses are like people, she said. If they are paid attention, they will perk up, even if they know they're not important, not making a contribution to architectural or social history, or even fashion, but simply are being noticed. The apartment was spacious and solidly constructed, dry in winter, cool in summer. Earlier attempts to modernise had not changed its essential nature, which was that it had been built in earlier times for a family.

She engaged a Polish house painter, whose artistic temperament was a check on her enthusiasms. He agreed under duress to paint their bedroom yellow over his preferred champagne, but only if it was oil not water based, which meant that they could not use the room for several nights. She forced a spa bath in the upstairs bathroom on a plumber who had been servicing the apartment block for years and did not believe there was enough space for it. To general applause, she reproduced a charming French tile she had used with effect in the bathrooms in Sydney. She had the kitchen rebuilt, replacing its clunky cupboards with slim lines and whirring machines. She wanted to replace the maize-coloured carpet downstairs with floorboards and was only dissuaded by the difficulty of choosing the right wood; the light woods were too pasty white, the dark woods were too hearty brown and the in-betweens, although enticing, had a pink tinge that did not match the already painted walls. She replaced the yellow satin curtains, which were supposed to match the maize carpet, choosing instead a cloth of striking pale orange threaded with white and green. She reorganised the terrace, placing some of her potted roses from Sydney in the most favourable, sunny positions, simplifying Mark's tangled impression of a garden with a more formal arrangement of urns in rectangles and triangles, heightened with a bamboo she had discovered that clustered and did not undermine foundations and interfere with the plumbing.

He enjoyed the physical companionship of marriage. He wanted her to know him as no one else did. He wanted her to draw from him the hope and passion he had concealed from others. For him, the public declaration of their relationship was a source of pride, but also relief. He had discovered himself, released from the habits of business rivalry and the family doctrine of keeping oneself at a distance. He subjected himself to Rukmini, confident that whatever it was she discovered in him, it would make no difference to their love of each other.

Their sleeping habits were different. She was composed and tidy, he was restless and disorderly. She slept silently, usually on her back, so that if he peeped at her during the night he saw only the outline of a mummy-figure with a small, tilted nose. He tossed and turned, threw off bedclothes, half-recovered them, buried his face in pillows, talked a lot. He often laughed in his sleep; when she heard it in the middle of the night, she was unsure whether to be amused or chilled. After several semi-sleepless nights she made her decision.

"I think we should sleep separately. I need a good eight hours, or I'm no good all day. And you're like a … willie wagtail. Willy-willy?"

She watched the effect on him for a moment, and then burst into laughter. "You know what I mean. Try saying it in Indonesian!"

Sometimes, if they were taking in separate bedrooms the afternoon siesta on which she insisted for herself and coerced him at weekends into imitating, she would unexpectedly pad into his room, half awake, her eyes seemingly closed, barely lifting her feet from the floor, guided by some internal direction finder to his bed. She would throw herself unerringly into a vacant space, snuggling into his curled-up shape, waking him from a slowly achieved, barely sustained semi-consciousness, and lapse immediately into an apparently profound state of sleep. When he was sure she was beyond recall, when her breath on his neck came steadily in delicious wafts of air, soundless and moist, he would extricate himself and sit at her side. Sometimes she would be fully clothed, except for shoes, with stockings wrinkled around her ankles. Sometimes, she would have discarded her outer garments and would now be lying on his bed only in underclothes and perhaps a blouse. He never ceased to be astonished and moved by her embodiment on his bed. Her body, exposed and secure, was living proof of their trust. Her slender fingers were clasped under her chin, her black hair swept back and held in place with one of her frilly elastic bands, her lips gently parted, the tip of her nose uplifted, as if in greeting, her ankles entwined, showing a couple of pink toes. He was overwhelmed with the simple dignity of the life he was sharing with her.

She woke with a slow unfolding, sitting up suddenly, often snapping at him in mock surprise.

"What are you doing here?"

Marriage was not the same process of self-discovery for Rukmini. She did not value the lengthy exchanges of confidences that he liked. She was uneasy with abstract truth. Her Javanese heritage told her that it was wise sometimes not to mention what you were doing, or intending to do, even wise perhaps to say that you were intending to do something entirely different from what you actually had in mind. Your actions were more likely to be successful if people had not been alerted to them in advance. Her double standard was not meant to be deceptive, even if she enjoyed any unintended benefits. Rather, she was following her father's maxim that public and private were different worlds. For her, the prime importance of marriage was in the public world: it meant social status and the production of children. Being married, as distinct from being a mistress, was as different as night from day, but it did not mean she had to tell him every little thing she was doing, or thinking of doing, and certainly not every little thing she was thinking. She did not like being asked to telephone him at a certain time, because she was not a punctual person, and it irritated her if, when she telephoned, he asked where she was or what she was doing. He, on the other hand, wanted to tell her everything. He was immensely satisfied, as if something had been achieved, when they bared the truth, the whole truth and nothing but the truth to each other.

Some of Rukmini's Indonesian female friends felt she had deserted them by marrying a foreigner, her Indonesian suitors were miffed and her father had difficulty accepting that another man was as important to her as himself. She treated former suitors with indifference and gently admonished her father. Deciding that her women friends were jealous, she regaled them with the news that if any woman could ever be satisfied by any man, she was that woman. She told everyone that she and Mark were made for each other, soulmates at one level and stunningly compatible at all others.

They imagined that as their sex life together had been so natural and lively, it would continue, with the inevitable and fortuitous result of pregnancy. It did not happen. She worked out precisely her fertile period each month and informed him of the dates. "There is a thirty-six hour window of opportunity," she announced. At the conclusion of each encounter she would prop herself on her shoulders, pedalling her legs in the air to assist in his sperm's penetration. After a few months of concentrated effort during these windows of opportunity without a result, she was concerned. She took medical advice; nothing of an "untoward nature" was apparent, a smiling doctor informed her. A facial rash developed, which bothered her. Then she made an embarrassing discovery. She had confused the beginning of menstruation with the end. So they began again, after she had placed on a bathroom wall a calendar with the vital windows circled in red. He said humorously that their libidinous natures might rebel against precursory attention, but she was adamant. It was necessary to get pregnancy "out of the way", so she could "get on" with the rest of her life. Her "biological clock" was ticking. She was no longer a "spring chicken".

"If we hadn't spent so much time thinking about getting married, instead of just doing it, we wouldn't be in this pickle," she said one night, with thoughtless inaccuracy.

He tried to be reassuring. "You'll become pregnant before you know it."

"Of course."

"Of course, what?"

"Of course I will be pregnant before I know it. I cannot know before it happens."

"But that's what you're trying to do. You're trying to will it."

She claimed to be puzzled by his logic. When she was puzzled by logic, she resorted to side effects.

"All my friends are having children." She produced a happy-mother photograph of a school friend and a bewildered baby face. "You would have never thought she wanted children. Now she has a lovely boy."

She had to make new friends in Melbourne. Women were wary of Rukmini. She enlisted them in causes that at the time of meeting they were not aware of, such as raising funds for a concert of Indonesian music or sending medical supplies to people injured in clashes with the Indonesian police or military. There was disagreement at times with her style. She ran the show, she made the decisions, she out-thought, out-manoeuvred and shouted down anyone who disagreed with her, so that her friendships with women were volatile. Mark ventured to appeal to her on behalf of an Indonesian woman who had received (verbally) the back of her hand. "She wants to be president of our group," Rukmini, who herself was president, said icily. "I had to show everyone she won't be."

She browsed in the stores for cold-weather clothes, choosing a navy blue overcoat, a thickly padded green-blue dressing gown, a grey, pink-flecked suit, a blouse with a high, checked collar and brown walking shoes. She had an old-fashioned belief that clothes were intended to conceal, not reveal. "Style is easy," she said, "you can make yourself look any way you want, but if you've really got it underneath, it's there to be discovered, isn't it?"

He showed her bits of Melbourne that had survived the crusaders of modernity and post-modernity, such as a tea house in The Block Arcade that stocked only leaves from Ceylon, and a coffee shop in an alley that ground your selection on the spot before serving. He wanted her to feel that she was in a place where survival did not depend on catching up with the latest global product, and the perpetual and anxious networking that was necessary to keep abreast of what others knew.

He was catching up with business developments, having neglected his interests while pursuing the interests of citizens of the new world order. He had been approached by investors in a new kind of airline, ferrying flowers, fresh fruit and vegetables to south-east Asia. With Rukmini at his side, he felt confident enough to try anything. Introducing her to Melbourne's modest antiquities was also a way of bringing her closer to him.

Rukmini's arrival in Melbourne was noticed by social hostesses. A beautiful Asian woman, descending from Australia's city of sin to surface in the heart of the Melbourne establishment, attached to a local businessman, handsome, athletic and, everyone had supposed, unyielding, was unlikely to pass unchallenged. Mark considered himself to be a man of the present, perhaps also of the future, and he was scornful of Melbourne's hostesses, who he thought were marooned in the past, unaware that cheap travel and digital entertainment had created another world. However, he looked for an opportunity to introduce Rukmini to his friends.

One of Melbourne's wealthiest families had endowed a foundation which brought notable speakers from abroad, funding a public lecture in the town hall and a reception afterwards downstairs in what was called the lower town hall. It was a high-minded cover for what was essentially a gathering of the city's social elite, not the most wealthy, nor the latest telegenic celebrities, but those with a desire for good works and the money and social standing to back it. He decided it was an appropriate occasion.

In earlier times, Melbourne's lord mayors had financed an annual ball. Held in the cavernous main hall decked out with streamers and coloured lanterns, and recuperated from at suppertime with refreshments in the lower town hall, its old-time atmosphere lingered, although the ball itself had succumbed to democratic politics and the allure of clubs and discotheques. Some who now repaired downstairs after the lecture, past vases of cannas and gladioli, had done so in their salad days after a succession of waltzes, foxtrots, schottisches and Gay Gordons. A distant excitement stirred again, trembling with memories of gloves above the elbow and tiny diaries with pencil attached, flowing gowns and white ties and tails.

Mark and Rukmini drifted around together, a man of distinction, dark and lean, although reticent and sometimes elaborately courteous, with a direct, appraising manner, inclined to stand still while others swirled about him, aware of who he was, modest yet forthright, but it was the fresh face beside him that attracted attention. Mark found himself hailed by men he scarcely knew, indeed, were sometimes so unknown that he had to ask them to introduce themselves to Rukmini, which they did with enthusiasm. Her high colour and inviting manner could be interpreted as flirtatious by men who were disposed to hope that it was. Several hostesses made fleeting contact, darting ingeniously through the male circle ("Where have you been keeping her?" and "Where did you acquire her?"). The men stood their ground, a phalanx of admiring cohorts, pressing those charms their experiences had proved to be reliable, expressing, in case charm proved ineffective, a serious interest in whatever Rukmini happened to be saying.

Her tendency to swing between frankness and timidity and her fluent, off-centre use of the English language led her into confusing, amusing situations. She described a man who had engaged her in a lengthy conversation as very "rude", which concerned Mark until she said he was "very rude for his age". She had encountered somewhere the phrase "in rude health".

A woman smiled at Mark and half-turned from her circle, inviting him to move across the room, which he did, detaching Rukmini from her admiring circle. She brushed his cheek with dry, facile lips in the accepted manner. She was Patricia, a handsome woman, who in an earlier century might have ridden her horse to the occasion and tethered it outside. She greeted Rukmini with a laughing aside, as if what she was saying was not for public consumption, although she would not care if it were overheard: "I've heard about you." She had a full range of teeth that she liked to display, while also enjoying the effect she had on people by turning down the corners of her mouth in studied appraisal. Rukmini smiled and waited. "We sit together at board meetings," said the woman, touching Mark's arm. "During the boring bits, we write notes to each other." "Oh," said Rukmini, wondering what he might have committed to writing. Not *The Bus Ride to Canberra*, surely. "Don't worry," said the woman. "Nothing to your detriment." She then embarked on a spirited critique of the lecture, which had been given by an English economist representing the new conservatism, which she characterised as "open slather and the devil take the hindmost". She spoke from the height of a Melbourne tradition of protecting local industry, with which her family had a long association.

A figure of importance greeted them, breaking through the assembly as if it were impeding his progress. He reached them almost out of breath and was introduced while he waited impatiently, smiling in recognition as each of his attributes was mentioned: city councillor, patron of the arts, businessman, lover of brilliant women. He accepted the final tribute as if it were no different from any other piece of information in his entry in Who's Who and beamed indiscriminately.

"At last we are getting culture back in Melbourne." Whether this was a reference to the occasion, the presence of their little group or to a future event of which he assumed they would be aware, was not clear. But he was flushed with the importance of whatever it was.

"I can't say that I was entirely in agreement with our speaker," said Patricia. Sincere, she was an interesting sight, her wonderful mouth neither gleaming nor resentful, her subdued features ordinary in the absence of wit and cunning. "I disapprove of what you say, but will defend to the death your right to say it!" the figure of importance announced. Pleased with his retort, he was galvanised by its implications. "The trouble with Melbourne is that it is too comfortable. We must cultivate our garden, of course, but the world is on the move, and we will be left behind if we don't catch up, sooner rather than later." He poised himself, as if he expected at any moment to bow to their applause, but Patricia chewed her lips to suppress a scathing retort and ruffled his hair, like an affectionate relative. "Go on with you." He retired from the contest without protest and Patricia gathered herself for departure.

"I hope to see more of you," she whispered to Rukmini, while kissing several cheeks in such rapid succession that the recipients found themselves brushing each other.

"So what did you make of it?" Mark inquired, as they travelled home by tram. He was a supporter of public transport and had early introduced Rukmini to Melbourne's trams, which she liked.

"I felt nervous," she said. "It wasn't that bad, was it?" he protested. "Melbourne has a quality," she said, staring ahead. "Like stuffy?" "No, not stuffy. Serious. It reminds me of Jogjakarta. Jakarta is like Sydney, anything goes. Do your own thing. Melbourne people are concerned about their culture, getting it right." "So if you like Jogja, which you do, you should like Melbourne?" he suggested. "I suppose so," she said, "but I'm used to living in anything-goes Sydney and thinking about culturally-correct Jogjakarta." She snuggled her head on his shoulder to end the conversation.

There was a full moon that night, flitting through the trees along St Kilda Road, and then suddenly as the tramlines swerved, low in the sky, big and shiny as a plate. When they got off the tram in Domain Road, Rukmini pointed to the parkland bordering the botanical gardens. "Why don't we make love on the grass with the moon looking down on us, pouring its energy into us?"

"It's too cold, we'd freeze."

"You're so sensible."

11

ONE NIGHT, AS THEY ATE snapper on the terrace of the Melbourne apartment, cooked in one of Rukmini's earthenware pots, and a red sky disappeared into twilight through the leaves of the elm tree next door, she told Mark she was sure her phone was tapped. "There's this click." She had a habit of folding her hands and looking solemn when she believed she had made a discovery confirming one of her suspicions, or contesting one of his. She had been convinced for some time that spies were encircling her and he had laughed at her fears.

"If they're my lot, it must mean budget allocations are due and if they're yours, they probably think you've gone over to the other side."

"They're yours, of course," she had retorted, drawing his attention to the obvious, which was that her Indonesian connections made it plausible that Australia's counter-intelligence agency would take an interest in her. In any case, her suspicions had been confirmed by another development. "A fellow in Canberra keeps ringing me for a lunch appointment."

"Bastards," Mark said amiably. He was not an admirer of the state and its secret agencies, which he liked to contrast with the relatively honest fraud and deception of the business world. The state had all the characteristics of a monopoly, including the tendency of those with a great deal of power to be alarmed by the prospect of anyone else having a tiny bit of it, and was deluded by the notion of its sovereignty, giving it a false moral authority. States seemed unable to compete peacefully in the world, elevating their petty rivalries to titanic and messianic struggles, invoking history and destiny, justifying the slaughter of people. In his heart, Mark agreed with E. M. Forster that he would rather betray his country than a friend, but he did not have the courage to do so, and he retreated from having to make the choice by the expedient excuse that it was not pressing in real life. Now, he knew that if he had to choose between betraying Rukmini and betraying his country, he would not betray her.

"Take it. See what he's like. Might be useful."

"But you can't stand them. Nor can I. Why should I bother with them?"

"A good question."

"And the answer?"

He did not know the answer. He did not want to try to understand the world of espionage, let alone play its game and obey its rules. He knew enough about it from hearsay to be confident that Australian agents could be trusted professionally, in the sense that they were competent. If the issues were terrorism or national security they would be experienced and capable, not on a fishing expedition. But he was also convinced that, like all bureaucracies, they were overweight and self-serving, anxious to find the evidence to justify their existence.

"Much of what they do is a waste of their time and everyone else's. When the Cold War ended, they were left without a prime target and they're scurrying around trying to keep their jobs by finding new ones. I'm sure some of them are genuine patriots, but you've got to assume a degree of corruption. They're human, after all. Some would be tempted to use professional information – like listening to you on the telephone – for personal, or political, effect. So the proper attitude to adopt to them is not fear, nor loathing, but disdain."

"That's very elegant, darling, but what's the action plan?"

He put down his fork, walked around the table and kissed her long and passionately. "That's my action plan."

Rukmini sometimes looked, as she did now, like a little girl whose Christmases had all come at once: she beamed, her eyes sparkling, her colour high, her lips pursed in appreciation of another kiss while, as the centre of attention, she also remained in strategic command.

"Thank you, but what's plan A?"

"Plan A is not to be disingenuous."

She put on her "Oh, yes, and what do you think that means?" face. She had been brought up to believe that facility in the English language was a mark of both education and intelligence, but her national pride and her personal conviction that content, not form, should count prevented her from pursuing efficiency in English. And at times Mark was irritatingly precise. When she was feeling relaxed and confident she would just ask for the meaning, but if she were tense she would screen her ignorance. So now she did not ask "What does that mean?" but "What do you think that means?" as if he had failed himself to be clear about what he was saying.

Mark took the hint. "I mean, we don't conceal our political opinions from them. Let them listen in to us, if they must. They might learn something about life. But be careful about information you have been given in confidence from the Indonesian side. Don't give them any interesting bits and pieces you've picked up, for example, from any of the East Timor factions. Their intention is twofold. First to get what they can from you and to provide you with information, or disinformation, which serves their purpose. If this seems to work, they might try to draw you in, even to recruit you."

"Recruit me! You're joking."

"They wouldn't want you to blow up bridges and steal documents. You'd be what's called an agent of influence. You'd be available to put their point of view."

"And what would I get out of it?"

"Official praise, protection and promotion. Security for the future."

Her father's daughter, she brushed these aside with a wave of her hand. "And what are our objectives in Plan A, mastermind?"

"Our objectives are to teach them about life. They have to be brought to realise that life outside the house of mirrors does not obey their rules, that not all relations between human beings are governed by the need to deceive, that while the state has the right to demand some allegiance it does not possess us body and soul. And we convince them that what they are doing in this case is a waste of their time and ours."

"We recruit them!"

"What job do you have in mind?"

"We recruit them into the ranks of the ...?"

"Secular, humanist, democratic, transparent, global citizenry."

"I love it when you say that." It was her turn to move around the table. "I think you're glorious!"

Emboldened, she met the man from Canberra for lunch regularly and reported to Mark about their meetings. "His name is ... Dug." She said it fondly, but she made it sound like mud. "First or second name?" "First, of course." "You mean Douglas?" "Maybe. He said it was ... Dug." She flipped her tongue when she said it, so it was not Doug, always Dug, with a flat finality about it that made its owner seem unusually earthbound, or stupid. Whenever Mark mentioned the man's name, he tried hard to make it sound the way she did, like mud.

"I quite like him," she reflected.

"That's a bad sign."

"I think he's unhappy."

"Well, he's in a dirty trade."

"Yes, but I think he feels it personally."

"What other way can you be unhappy?"

"His family life is a bit wobbly, but I think it's alright. No, I think he wants to get out of what he's doing, but it's hard, once you get into that sort of business."

Mark looked at her with mixed admiration and concern. "Don't tell me you've turned him!"

"What does turning mean?"

"He wants to get out of the room of mirrors and join the rest of us in this rackety old world of love and hate and murder and mayhem."

"Maybe." She was not yet ready to take credit, but neither was she prepared to brush off the suggestion. She was in a "deep pond", not yet ready to surface.

"Darling, that's fantastic. How did you do it?"

"I don't know." She seemed genuinely perplexed. "I just talked about life and the universe."

When Rukmini spoke in this innocent manner it was difficult to know whether she was being honest or disingenuous. Mark decided to let her encounter with Dug take its course. "Well, keep me posted."

Crossing the Arafura Sea

※

A week later she folded her hands demurely at the dinner table and he knew that some news was about to break.

"I think he's in trouble. Dug. They want to send someone else from Canberra to have lunch with me. They don't think he's getting anywhere with me."

"They're probably right."

"He says they think he's fallen for me."

Mark experienced a tremor of jealousy, stifled in favour of common sense. "Maybe he has."

"No, we've just become good friends. We talk about all sorts of things he's interested in. He's really a spiritual person, not political at all. He's no good at Canberra's bureaucratic in-fighting. And his marriage is not really spiritual. His wife is very practical, and not especially social, either. He's very attached to the children, and wishes he could spend more time with them."

"Hmm. What else?"

"Well, not much, really."

"You don't talk about East Timor? Or illegal fishermen? Or the political disposition of students? Or who's going to get this and that appointment in the Indonesian military? Or whether ..."

"We talk about other things. We agree on politics in general. So we don't really talk about it." She had a faraway look in her eyes.

"I can see why Dug's being replaced. They send him all the way down from Canberra for an expensive lunch, and all you give him is the birds and the bees."

She shrugged her shoulders. "It won't do them any good."

She was as good as her word, taking an instant dislike to the new man from Canberra, who compounded their mistake by trying immediately to put pressure on her. She refused to make an appointment with him for another lunch. She would only talk to Dug, she said, flipping her tongue. They told her that he had been transferred. She confirmed this by meeting him secretly in Canberra. He took her to his home to meet his wife and children. They became friends. Eventually, the contact with the Australian

Security Intelligence Organisation (ASIO), which is what it had been, lapsed.

Rukmini maintained that the outcome was proof that human beings had more in common than political parties, governments or the state would acknowledge. Mark's astonishment at her achievement was encapsulated in what became known as *The Turning of ASIO*, the details of which he would report to friends with delight.

Part Three

12

THEY WERE SOPHISTICATED AND COSMOPOLITAN, successful and accomplished in the ways of the world, yet both were tied by umbilical cords to lives that were simple and frugal. Beneath their passions, ambitions and ideals, they were aware of a simple core in life of suffering and survival. Each knew it was important that their relationship did not neglect this core, gliding over it in pursuit of pleasure and invention. Mark asked Rukmini to come with him to the farm where he had lived as a boy.

They travelled by car from Melbourne for five hours along thin, straight roads over flat farmlands, except that the road, executed, if not planned, by pragmatists who followed the lay of the land rather than a strategic vision, would without warning dip and dart into shelter patches of trees, wind through speckled creek beds, and then rise and break out into broad sunlight and another long straight run to the horizon. The panorama was not of the quality that had delighted her on the highlands between Sydney and Canberra, nor the spectacular sweep of green and gold fields that greeted her as she drove from Lorne through the Otways, suddenly emerging from the forest as you reach the Colac road leading to Deans Marsh. She did not exclaim that this was her highway to freedom. This was the Mallee, a sombre, subdued Australian countryside, not marginal but hard-worked, not forbidding but not welcoming either. This was practical, down-to-earth country. No extras, like fence lines of imported poplars or cedars, or homesteads with tiled or painted roofs and cypress hedges, but rather a simplicity that gave a surprising impression of untidiness. Paddocks edged and subsided into each other, dead trees had not been removed, abandoned machinery rusted unnoticed, truck tyres were left where they had deflated. Nothing is more desolate than a stationary windmill with broken sails. She watched silently, and then fell asleep.

He took her to the one-teacher school where he had learned to read, write and add up long columns of figures (all valuable in later life, he assured her), the wheat silo where he had worked as a weighbridge clerk on summer holidays, the general store which still had the same smell of oil and leather with a faint overlay now of breakfast foods, the all-purpose hall where the school end-of-the year concert was held.

He sang for her (in a Peter Dawson baritone) as he had sung, with corks dangling from one of his father's hats. He danced with her, as he had once danced, on the old, polished, hardwood floor, after which, on one knee and hand on heart, he sang, as he had once sung (in prepubescent soprano).

This was the hall where he had slid up and down on wheat bags, rope-hauled by young men over boards strewn with the scrapings of candles to wax the floor for dancing. This was where Aunt Joan had "danced the night away" with a married man, creating a scandal (or so her mother thought). They had skimmed over the shining floor like ice-skaters, dance after dance, laughing and smiling with pleasure at each other, looking into each other's eyes, their hands and arms intimately entwined, no hint of a trip or a misjudged movement, such a perfect match that local gossip was instantly kindled. He recounted how, according to Chandler family lore, Aunt Joan had been wakened by her mother before cockcrow on the morning after the dance.

"Something will happen to you, my girl, if you dance like that."

"For God's sake, Mum, like what?"

"Like that with Whatshisname."

"We just danced, Mum, like everyone else."

"It was not like everyone else."

"You mean we danced better than anyone else. That wouldn't be difficult."

"Don't get smart with me. You know what I mean. You should be studying, not gallivanting around the dance floor."

"It was a dance, Mum. What was I supposed to do. Take a book?" And so on.

In buoyant spirit, they reached the white hill and then the red hill, which seemed now only inclines in the road, not the mountains of his boyhood, and the property they had journeyed to see stretched out before them. He explained how he had walked to school each day, how he had carefully chosen a stick to push along in front of him, needing to assess the right length and spring, the right shape of head that would plough through the dust and the hard stone ridges in summer or the puddles and mud patches in winter, so that by the time he reached school it had been worn to a shining point that slid over the ground as smoothly as a snake's head. He showed her the quandong bushes with their brilliant red fruit – the sharp tasting skin around a pockmarked nut the size of a marble. He took her to an innocent flat section of the road where he had had to fight his way, in a manner of speaking, against a patrolling snake, its body arched like the figurehead in the bows of a galleon, its eyes glinting fiendishly, its head poised to strike.

He steered the car off the main road, across a level railway crossing, through a clump of trees that had once been an entrance and turned into … nothing. The house, the stable, the wool shed, the cow bail, the chicken run, the pig sty, the machinery shed had all gone. Only the dam remained, a decline of yellow mud. He walked away from her silently, striding across paddocks that he remembered as brown, furrowed earth, now a flat surface of hardy grasses. Where his father had cultivated prize-winning new varieties of wheat was now fenced off, barren except for ravaged water troughs. He surveyed the landscape where once harvesters had paraded in stately progress in clouds of chaff and dust, now bare. He returned to where the house had been and wandered alone over the plot of weeds that had been his playground, the cellar where boxes of apples had been kept fresh, now collapsed on itself, the water tank, now just a rubble of stumps and rusted hoops, the back verandah, where he had read tales of mystery and imagination, with a plate of apples under his bed, now only decomposed sheets of galvanised iron. When she joined him, she could see that his eyes were filled with tears. She put an arm around him.

"Remember Lake George!"

"It's alright. It's not me I'm feeling for, it's a little, barefoot boy. I can even remember what was in his head. Dreams of adventure, glory and romance. Well ..." He shrugged as if the dreams had evaporated, but she tightened her arm. "They've all come true!" He patted her hand, but she would not be put off, holding him tightly, and then darting off, propelled suddenly by the sight of something, returning with it held aloft in one hand.

"Darling! Do you remember?"

He examined a rusty iron hinge. It might have been from a gate, but had a solid shape, with a trace of oil under the flaking surface, suggesting that it was from a truck or tractor or perhaps a piece of agricultural machinery, like a harvester.

"Let's keep it. You might have touched it sometime."

"Maybe." He was doubtful.

"Anyway, it's a good idea to keep something like this. It helps the grieving."

"I'm thinking about my father," he said, as they walked back to the car with their arms around each other's waists. "He put so much into this place. He wanted it to be a model for the district, scientific farming, the right seed of wheat and the right breed of sheep for this climate and this soil. Gimlet farming, he called it. Lean, sparing and strong. Now, it's obviously just being run as part of another property."

Mark was deeply grateful for Rukmini's presence on that visit. He knew he would have been depressed if he had been alone, or even if he had been there with other members of the family. She was so lovely, and so alive, that her presence was thrilling, standing in the debris of his father's hopes and his own dreams. Anything was possible with her at his side. He knew then that he wanted her to be with him for the rest of his life.

And something more. Was it too extravagant to think that they might be able to move history, that they might be able to show the doubters, the racists, the one-eyed Aussie nationalists and the hooded Indonesian militarists that these two vastly dissimilar societies, forced to become not just geographical neighbours but also historical partners, could demonstrate to the world what the values of the new millennium might be. If the royal families of old Europe could make their marriages to suit the political convenience of their countries, why could not citizens of the new secular, humanist, democratic world order make decisions about marriage with their national interests in mind? A love match that served the interests of their two countries was a powerful double.

They went to one of Warracknabeal's 19th century hotels in the hope that he might see a face or hear a name that would jog his memory, but it was early afternoon and a gloomy bar, smelling of carbolic phenol, was empty except for a couple of city folk like themselves. They had been to see a local tourist attraction, which they discussed with an elderly man behind the bar as he leisurely pulled the draught levers to serve them two glasses of beer. They had been to the top of an outcrop of rock from where you could see across miles and miles of "well, nothing, really". The experience had been nevertheless exhilarating in some way they could not explain. "Actually you can see some salt lakes in the distance." When they had gone, after promising that they would be back for another visit, Mark asked the barman if he had known his father, or heard of him.

"Yeah, I've heard of him. Good left-hand batsman, killed in the war."

He seemed unable to raise his eyes to Mark's face, or perhaps he was trying to avoid looking at Rukmini. His own face was a study in disenchantment as Mark explained that as a small boy he had grown up not far from where they were.

"So you've gone to live in the city."

The man spoke as if he were required to accept one of life's bitter lessons. His lowered eyes and persistent wiping of a towel on the bar's surface added animus to everything he said. "Not many left around here from those days."

"Yes," said Mark, "I was wondering ..."

"You'd have to have nothing between the ears to stay on," the man said. His attitude to the bar's surface was a mix, obviously unresolved, of fondness and contempt. He ran the towel smoothly over it with an almost sensual carefulness, and then suddenly brushed it with a sweep that unsettled glasses and brought a flush of colour to his face.

"Yeah," said Mark, taking on the host's laconic style but deciding to ignore the possibility that those who had remained were, in the barman's opinion, brainless. "Any still around?"

"I suppose you're married now, and everything." The towel was flying back and forth like a shuttlecock. While Mark stumbled for an answer, the man raised his eyes to Rukmini's face for the first time. No longer hooded, his eyes were surprisingly soft, although still only half open. They were hurt eyes, eyes that had seen terrible things, although it was unlikely that he had been responsible for the terror; they were not guilty eyes. He looked at her in a tender daze, as if she were an embodiment of hopes and dreams now come to haunt him. Then he disentangled a large hand from the towel and extended it across the table.

"Pleased to meet you. I'm Bill."

Bill and Rukmini discovered a subject of mutual interest. If it weren't for tourism, according to Bill, business would be much worse than it was. People from all over the state, sometimes interstate, came in busloads. "The rocks here are just the right height. If they were any higher, people wouldn't be able to climb them." He smiled knowingly, as if the height had been determined by some local authority with an uncanny knowledge of the climbing ability of city folk. But (knowingness now replaced by openness, with a countryman's acceptance of wonder) it wasn't just tourists. Scientific people came from the cities, even from overseas, digging for fossils and looking for rock paintings.

"The place is alive out there with people scratching around," said Bill. "They come in here asking all kinds of questions." The knowing look returned. "Especially about the, well, you know, indigenous people. How they're treated, that sort of thing." His face was unsure whether to register shame or pride.

As an enthusiastic traveller, Rukmini saved him the torment of a decision, agreeing with him about the benefits of tourism and imparting her knowledge of famous tourist attractions. He listened courteously. "Go on," he said, nodding in what could be either wonderment or disbelief. "Of course, the people here don't just want to be tourist objects," he said, as if to check the direction in which Rukmini seemed to be heading. "We've got a few ideas. Community centre. A cooperative store. That kind of thing. If we wait on the commercial fellows, we'll be here till doomsday. We're not a commercial proposition. Too small. So we're thinking about it ourselves. I'm on a couple of committees."

You could not tell from his face, which had developed over time a sheath of impassivity, or from his troubled eyes whether the committees were a valuable source of local energy or a waste of everyone's time. Then he turned to Mark, extending his hand again.

"Sorry about that. I was just being a bit careful. As I said, people come in here asking all sorts of questions. Of course, I knew your father." He observed Mark for a long time as if he was trying to put that knowledge into a perspective that was appropriate to present circumstances.

"I met him on the wharf at Souda Bay. He was an officer and I was a private, and I didn't know whether to salute him. The last time we had met was at the old government water tank up the road here. We had both gone up to check whether it was full. It was very quiet up there, like it always is, and it was only the two of us. I remember him saying, "Finding another person up here is like disturbing someone at prayer." He was an unusual man, your father. But on the wharf it was hustle and bustle, gear everywhere, people shouting. It was hard to find a quiet spot to talk. I had been in Greece. We were being evacuated. You father had just arrived, facing it for the first time. So I felt I should give him a few wrinkles. I told him about the mines. I hated the mines. They were everywhere. I couldn't fathom the mine-layers, they weren't fighters, they were exterminators, like we are with rabbits, laying the damn things all over the place, catching old people, women and children, anyone. But they were lazy, always leaving them in nice easy soil to dig, like loam, so you could pick where they were and you were safe if you walked on hard, high, dry ground. I told all this to you father. And, then, of course, there were the paratroopers."

He raised his soft, hooded eyes to Mark, and then to Rukmini. "I didn't see him for a while and I thought a paratrooper must have got him. They were something new. Suddenly the sky would be full of them, floating down like snow, silent, landing quietly, saying nothing to each other, just turning quickly and all moving in the same direction, as if they had been programmed, like robots."

Mark inserted some family history. "He had organised a digging party on one side of a field and was walking back across it to board a coastal vessel that needed repairs after a German bombing raid the day before."

"In the middle of a paddock, was it?" said Bill. "They loved landing in paddocks. He was lucky to get out alive."

For Mark, this man was as important a witness to the life of his father as might be found. He was outside the family and its enclosed mythology, sensitive to country life and perhaps to whatever it was that had drawn his father to it, and there, on the wharf at Souda Bay, on an ancient, fabled island, his father had shared with him thoughts on life and death.

"What was your opinion of him? My father."

Bill looked up quickly, his eyes almost fully opened. "Don't you worry. He would have given a good account of himself, in the circumstances. He was very fit. He had a good eye and quick hands. But he was badly wounded, left in the field for dead and when he finally got back to Australia, he never really settled down."

"Yes," said Mark. "But I was thinking of something else. The kind of man he was, in general."

"In general?" Bill's towel took a wide sweep, and then a vigorous rubbing of a well polished section. "That's something, isn't it? A tall order, in general." He behaved as if either he had not fully understood the question and did not want to admit it, or that the question itself was tactless, probing sensitivities not normally revealed in polite conversation in his social circle. "But I can say this. People admired your father."

"I know that," said Mark, almost crossly. "But what kind of man was he?"

The rubbing slowed to a few inconclusive movements, as Bill reorganised his defences against the savagery of this inquisition. Why was this man so anxious for another's opinion of his father? Rukmini smiled encouragingly at him and his confidence lifted.

"Well, I'll say this. He was different from his father, your grandfather. Old Tom was a humdinger. With Tom Chandler, well, you had to watch it. Straight, but competitive. Very competitive. Your father wasn't at all like that. In some ways, he didn't think of himself on the same level as everyone else. He accepted everyone was different and he liked finding a way of smoothing over the differences. He was the best captain of the district cricket team we ever had. Of course, being a left-hand batsman, he was different. He was hard to bowl to. If you were just a little bit off-line, he would tickle the ball around the leg side, or cut you behind point. He could drive, too, straight down the ground, no power, just timing. But he was a good captain because he knew the strengths and weaknesses of every member, whether they were good with the bat or the ball or in the field, and he balanced them up to make the team stronger as a whole. My dad always said he should have been a politician."

"Yes, that's what everyone says," said Mark. He seemed disappointed, as if he had heard this account of his father too often, and had been hoping to discover that he was not what everyone said he was. "Is that good?"

Bill, relieved, joined in the laughter. "Depends on who you talk to around here," he said. "There's good politicians, who want to help the farmers and the rural towns, and there's bad politicians, who are in with the big cities and foreign capital. That's about it."

"Of course, it's good," Rukmini exclaimed. She had decided that she knew how to handle Bill and it was time for her to take over. Her instinct for knowing when she was liked or disliked was quick and usually sure, and she had learned to distinguish between a response to her looks, which was likely to be short-lived (although still useful at times) and acceptance of her at a more serious level. She had decided that she and Bill were communicating with each other at this other level, and she was right. Within a few minutes, a transformation had taken place. Bill put a "Back in half an hour" sign on the door, and they were joined by Audrey, his wife, a handsome, white-haired woman bearing a tray with a teapot, four cups and saucers and a plate of biscuits.

She led them to a table in the non-smokers' section. "We had to have a non-smokers' once the tourists started coming. Of course, many of the locals have stopped smoking, too." She was a prim, attentive woman with a quick walk and a humorous shrug to her shoulders. "The radio talk-back goes on and on about being politically correct," she said, arranging the contents of the tray on the table, "but it seems to me it's just a matter of courtesy. If you're in business, you soon learn that every customer is different and you have to avoid giving offence to anyone." She rolled her eyes at her husband. "Of course, some would still prefer to treat everyone as if they are all the same."

Rukmini's sensitivity to the genetics of skin was highly developed. Something about the texture of Audrey's skin, her features and the way she moved prompted the thought that she was of Aboriginal descent.

Somehow, in a way that only Rukmini knew how to do, the thought, less than suspicion but more than conjecture, was projected and confirmed, openly and happily. Within minutes, the two women were engaged in an intense exchange of confidences, while the two men talked about the weather and farming and why Bill had sold the property that his father had tried for so long to develop and bought the hotel, which made good money and was a way of keeping in touch, through the customers, with what was going on. The women were single-minded in their personal discovery of each other. The men examined each other under the cover of life's events, keeping an ear cocked to what the women were saying.

Audrey's story was that she had been adopted, believing that she was a natural daughter until after she married Bill, when she was told the truth. They had two children, a boy, who now had his own building business in Kerang, and a girl, who was a nurse in Melbourne. She had told the children when they were still teenagers.

"But I didn't know at that stage who my real mother was. I just said I'd been adopted and everyone accepted it, as if it didn't matter."

When the law was changed, so that you could find out who your real parents were, she had thought about it for a long time. What was the point in finding out? She and Bill had been through a lot together, the war, the children, deciding to give up the farm and take the pub. They knew everyone in the district and were accepted as longstanding members of the community. Why bother? She didn't want to change anything. She didn't want to draw attention to herself in any way. She fitted in. What did it matter who her parents were? She was who she was, whoever they were.

"But somehow I couldn't resist it. It wasn't that I was unhappy, or that I wanted to prove something, or that I hoped I would find I was the discarded child of someone famous, or anything like that." She looked at Rukmini with her warm, brown, searching eyes as if she was seeking consolation, or approval. "It was just ... wanting to know." She laughed. "For the first time in my life, I understood the real meaning of Eve's temptation in the Garden of Eden."

"And you found her?"

"Yes, I did."

"And ...?"

Audrey's manner had undergone several changes since she brought in the tea things. She had dropped the chatter that protected her, throwing herself into the excitement of a tete-a-tete with Rukmini, her striking features animated, her eyes sparkling and darting. Now that she was facing truths about herself, and something much bigger, truths about her community, her country (even the human race), her shoulders slumped and her features subsided, although her voice remained strong, as if she were determined that it would be unaffected.

"It was a bit of a shock," she said, sighing. "I had grown up in such a different way. I was hardly aware that Aboriginal people existed. Then, there's my mother!" Her eyes sought Rukmini's again. "Well, she was quite old, of course."

"Yes, of course." Rukmini could see it all, and held back. What was the point in squeezing out the last drop of reality, the ragged clothes, the mournful eyes, the sagging flesh? "And is she still alive?"

"Oh no. Quite a while ago."

"Oh, well," said Rukmini, as if that might be a blessing in disguise. She leaned across and squeezed Audrey's hand. "And are the children happy?" They were, yes, very happy, doing extremely well. She said "extremely" as if her emphasis made some quantitative difference that would be appreciated. But ... Audrey made a movement as if to withdraw her hand, and then allowed it to remain. She raised her eyes and they were like pools of despond. Rukmini guessed instantly the source of her trouble: the children had not been told who her real mother was.

"I couldn't do it to them. I brought them into the world. They had no choice about that but, now, well ..." She had not withdrawn her hand and the two women leaned towards each other so that their hands could remain locked across the table. "There's so much nastiness about. And they're not really ... I mean, my father was a white man. They're hardly Aboriginal at all. Why bother them with it? They might do something silly, like take up a cause, or throw themselves into being Aboriginal. But I just want them to be happy, have a normal life. That's what they're entitled to, don't you agree?"

Rukmini was silent.

"Perhaps you would know that yourself?"

Rukmini laughed, withdrew her hand, sat up straight, looked about her, smiled at Mark as if he had already heard what she was about to say.

"They should get on with their lives, ignore all the nastiness. Those people are like children, calling each other names. Ignore them."

Audrey was relieved to have her burden lifted. "You can say that again!" She was so pleased to have the company of an outsider who understood her predicament and could be cheerful about it that she suggested they might like to stay overnight. But Rukmini had become noticeably thoughtful and Mark had reached the limits of his conversation with Bill, who was looking uneasily in his wife's direction.

Mark and Rukmini supported each other's explanation of the need to stay overnight nearer to Melbourne, so that they could meet urgent commitments the following morning, so they parted in a flurry of handshakes, kisses, waves and promises of return.

In the car, Rukmini told Mark what it would have been like for Audrey, discovering her real mother. "It was probably in a camp on the outskirts of some country town. She'd be sitting there in the middle of kerosene tins and dogs and snotty kids, probably not a tooth in her head, likely barefoot, smoking a fag, crazy looking." She looked across at him angrily. "It's a scandal the way they are, the way they've been treated."

"They've certainly had the rough end of the stick," said Mark.

"What's that supposed to mean? They don't have any bit of the stick, smooth, rough or anything in between. They're just nothing, outcasts. If white Australians spent half as much on giving the Aborigines a decent living as they spend on food and shampoo for their dogs and cats and bird seed for their budgerigars, Australia would be a much better place."

Later, when he thought she would have calmed down, Mark said, "What a fluke, meeting Bill like that."

"What is a fluke?"

"A lucky accident."

"It was no fluke. It was destiny."

Mark knew better than to challenge her on probability theory, but he did say, "You and Audrey seemed to get along very well."

"We are sisters," Rukmini retorted, looking straight ahead. "Sisters." Later still, she aroused herself from dozing and announced, "But I think she was wrong, not telling the children. The bottom line is, she's ashamed. That's why she didn't tell them, and she shouldn't be ashamed." Rukmini seemed to be arguing with herself. "She shouldn't be."

"It's hard on him," said Mark, "knowing, but having to keep it from the children."

"Oh, well." Rukmini was not in the mood for sympathy. "He's alright. She's a great asset for him. In any case, I'm not sure he knows. She never said anything about telling him." She gave the impression that if a distinction were to be made between telling the children and telling the father, the former weighed more heavily on her conscience.

"Surely she would have told him," Mark suggested, in all reasonableness.

"You can't be sure."

"No, but if it was you, you would, wouldn't you?"

"You know I tell you everything."

On that happy note, the journey continued. Rukmini would say later that Mark had shown himself to her with a depth of emotion and what she called "life's bare truth" that he had not done before. All she had known of his father was that he had given up trying to run the farm, had gone into business and had died while Mark was still a boy. Now she could see a connection between Mark's search for success in business and his need to discover the true quality of the father he had scarcely known. But it had been as much a journey of discovery for her as for him. In their international travels, she had felt that he was part of a global elite, using business skills and the English language, making assumptions from its own experience about what was economic growth and what was social progress, while she was part of a global mass, struggling to keep its head above the poverty line by any means available, urgently in need of quick results whatever the socio-economic model that produced them. The contradiction in this model of their relationship, which gave it a humorous twist appreciated by them both, was that she was aristocratic by temperament while he was democratic. He appreciated her position rather more than she appreciated his. The compound of success and humility in his position was irritating, despite her best intentions, so she was pleased to find in his past an imperfection for which she could offer condolence.

She kept the iron hinge, and shortly afterwards she gave Mark a small, round silver container, like a snuff box. He examined the detail of the lid, rubbed a finger around its circumference, pondered its utility.

"Open it."

Inside was a brown, friable substance like dry tobacco. Before he could touch or sniff it, she explained: "It's from the soil of my Javanese grandfather's grave."

She asked him if he would come with her father and herself on their next visit to the ancestral graveyards.

"If you want to understand me, which I admit is a challenge ..."

"Please thank your father." He was extremely formal.

"You won't have to sleep in the graveyards with us. I'll put you in a motel."

"You're very thoughtful."

"Of course, if you want to sleep with us, you can. But it wouldn't mean much to you, would it?"

"Sleeping with you always means a lot to me."

"Be serious for once."

"You say I'm always serious."

"I mean be serious for once about something you're not serious about."

13

A SMALL TOWN ON THE south coast of Java, Pacitan, had been fixed in Rukmini's mind since she was a little girl, the site of her family, a community that, modestly endowed, was struggling in modern Indonesia to survive and which she and her father were committed to protect and nurture. As head of the clan, Haryo strove from the vantage of Jakarta to keep up his reputation as a professional and business man who knew how the real world worked, which was not easy for him as he had renounced comfort and lived austerely. He meditated daily, did not bother with access to current events and information, such as having a radio or television set, or reading the newspapers, and relied on the telephone and conversation with his many friends, who visited frequently but were not always well-informed. His sister, Haryati, and her husband, Totok, presided over the clan on site.

Relations between Rukmini and her aunt were governed by speculation about what would happen if Haryo died. He was obviously preparing Rukmini for a role in the family, but it would be unusual for a single woman to become head of the clan. In the normal way, her aunt and uncle would succeed to the title, but they had no money and these days money was essential. In the old days, your position itself ensured that you had enough to keep up appearances. There was always a house and your food was somehow provided. These days, the position itself was powerless. It only became effective if you had the means to maintain it. This was modern

Indonesia, of which Haryo was disdainful, so that even as he shared his declining knowledge of the workaday world, he preferred to live in the past and was inclined to keep Pacitan in a similar state. During the year, he kept a light rein on clan affairs from Jakarta. Any misfortune, such as serious illness requiring time in hospital, he was expected to pay for, or at least to lead in encouraging subscription from others. Sometimes he was persuaded to help finance some (usually unsuccessful) project. Occasionally, he would visit in what might be called an unofficial capacity. But the annual pilgrimage with Rukmini to pray in the ancestral graveyards was the commanding event in the clan's calendar, in obedience to which all its priorities fell into place.

Haryati suspected that her brother had put aside in his will an amount which would enable her niece to take over as leader of the clan. In addition, Rukmini had an income of her own, had graduated from an Australian university and had some influence in Jakarta because of her job, all of which created an aura of lustre and authority. "She will watch me all the time," Rukmini had confided to Mark, as they discussed the Pacitan visit in their Jogjakarta hotel, which he was now sorry to be leaving, so entranced had he become with the gamelan music in the foyer. The sedate and patient players, their minds concentrated on the music, or elsewhere, would have seemed like spirits, were it not for their nut-brown and indigo-blue, buttoned-up costumes, as formal as uniforms, and the golden tone and beat of the music which, although mesmeric, was earthy, not celestial.

"She will notice the eye shadow and the transparent nail polish, the moist, orange-red lipstick, the pearl necklace and earrings. She will talk about my appearance after we've gone. Even when I used to try to be just a Pacitan girl, she would talk about me as if I were a foreigner, so I gave up. Now I present myself as a woman of the world."

They were accompanied by her younger sister, a plumper and sulkier version of the family's genetic code, who was not pleased to be riding into the night and in retaliation immediately fell asleep. Her father sat in front with the driver and slept, too, or might have been in a trance so little attention did he pay them, or anyone or anything else. They dozed and jostled together in the four-wheel drive hired for the occasion, which had met them at Jogjakarta airport; eventually Rukmini put her feet up and using Mark's lap as a pillow also slept. Upright in the night, he alone kept the driver company as Indonesia slipped past, a blur of trees and dimly lit villages.

As there were no bypass roads, they would occasionally enter a town, crawl along a main street clogged with traffic and pedestrians, under coloured lights, advertising and political banners. Between towns, they were from time to time forced to negotiate road space with a succession of lumbering trucks lit up like showboats. Mark imagined an accident in which by mouth-to-mouth resuscitation he saved the father's life and for which Rukmini was forever in his debt.

It was nearly midnight when they arrived in Pacitan. Their vehicle moved slowly through the deserted streets, as if trying not to be noticed, but the lights at the house were still on. They crept into the big front yard, crunched over pebbles, stopped. The driver switched off the lights, cut off the engine, rested his head on the steering wheel. Inside was dark and silent. Haryo unwound himself, stretched his arms, lifted his legs one after the other, descended. He stood on the ground and arched his back, and then spoke softly towards the back of the vehicle.

"We're here."

He smiled lightly through his tiredness, leant over, touched and shook gently his sleeping daughters, nodded at Mark. Then he spoke quickly and sharply to the driver, who went to the back and unloaded boxes and bags.

"Why can't we sleep here?" The voice of the sister was husky and irritable.

"Don't be silly. They're waiting for us."

The silence in the back now had a different quality, suggesting a reappraisal. "They're still up?"

"Of course."

"God, they must be mad."

"It is their custom," the father said. "They have been doing it all their lives. Why should they stop just because we are running a bit late?"

They spoke in the national language, Bahasa, sometimes in Javanese. Every now and then they would speak or translate in English for Mark's benefit. "Dutiful daughter number two reporting for duty," the sister said, and saluted. Dutiful daughter number one took Mark by the hand. "Just stand there looking gorgeous. I'll keep an eye on you." She swung her handbag over her shoulder and stalked towards the house. She looked through a window and motioned them excitedly with one hand. Through the window, they could see people stretched out asleep. Some were curled up on sofas and had covered themselves with blankets. Some, also covered, were lying on the floor. Two were slumped in chairs, like delayed passengers at an airport, their faces open to the world.

"The welcoming committee."

Rukmini went to the door, which was not locked, and opened it gently, giving a subdued rat-tat-tat on the wood to announce their arrival. The tableau sprang into life. As their feet groped, searching for sandals, their eyes swung to the four figures in the doorway. They rose as one and flocked towards the father, touching daughter number one as they passed but concentrating their full attention on him.

"You've come!"

"You're here!"

They touched him several times, running their fingers down his arm or his shirt front. A woman caressed his cheek.

"And how is my brother?"

Her voice was louder than needed. Her words were a reminder to the welcoming committee that she was in charge.

"We are all well, Haryati," he said, indicating his daughters. "We have brought a friend from Australia," he added, vaguely indicating the presence of Mark. "We are all a bit tired. The plane was late into Surabaya. Then we had a small accident on the road."

The possibility that the father had read his mind flickered in Mark's consciousness, but he realised this was merely social dissimulation, avoiding an apology for having kept everyone waiting so long. There had been no accident, big or small. It was not clear why they had arrived in the middle of the night. They had spent time in Jogjakarta that might have been better spent on the road. The plane had not been late and, in any case, they had come from Jogjakarta, not Surabaya. But it was hardly his business nor, prudently, his prerogative, to point this out. "Don't bother with one, two and three," Rukmini had said, meaning to be helpful. "Just go with the flow."

However, the road map surrounding Pacitan was one of the few certainties about the outside world of which the clan's knowledge was assured.

"You came through Kediri or Madiun?" As they had come through neither, which were major towns on the way from Surabaya, but instead through a network of smaller roads leading from Jogjakarta, Haryo merely smiled. A modest argument broke out among the men on the merits of each approach, including the key role in either of a small but interconnected town, Ponogoro. Haryo continued to smile, as if he were presiding over a debate and would shortly announce the winner. "Wonosari," Rukmini announced, with a certain impatience. "Ah! Wonosari." The faces turned to her in wonderment and the name of the town was repeated, like a tolling bell. "Wonosari!"

"So you came from Jogja?"

"Yes."

"Ah!"

"A small accident?"

"Yes, those roads are very bad."

The mystery of Surabaya and the delayed plane, the merits of Madiun and Kadiri, as well as the motives of the clan's leader in deliberately misleading them, not to mention those of his daughter in abruptly correcting him, were allowed to evaporate in the welcome confirmation of the notoriously unserviceable roads connecting Pacitan to Wonosari.

The chorus of anguish and disapproval was unanimous. "Terrible roads!"

Haryati sidled up to her brother with a reproachful glance. "Why are you angry with me?" She asked as if she were a little girl seeking forgiveness, pouting and leaning her head on one side.

"Angry?" He was perplexed.

"You are so formal." She continued to pout, reproaching him with her eyes.

He laughed away her inquisition, as if it were not to be taken seriously. Everyone except Haryati laughed with him and the girls smiled carefully.

"Well, let's eat."

Rukmini moved to her father's side as they walked towards a table laden with dishes.

"You used her full name."

"Oh, that." He laughed again.

He looked handsome when he laughed. His dark skin stretched tight, his eyes flashed, the seriousness of his purpose in life was for a moment made light. They were infected by his laughter and clustered around, waiting for him to choose something to eat. When he did, they followed him, complimenting him on his choice, rather than his sister for having created the dish, although she was quick to remark on the splendour of the feast laid out for them again this year. Actually, Rukmini whispered to Mark, it was the same as last year. It was always like this – not a feast really, just a few "enticements", as Haryati always said.

"Just a few enticements," said Haryati on cue.

The sister wandered around the table, picking at bits and pieces.

"Everything under control?"

It was not really a question. The father offered it rather as an all-purpose comment, which took account of the fact that they were all here again this year and that, presumably, arrangements for activities the following day had been satisfactorily made. A chorus responded.

"Oh, yes! Everything under control."

A man in a sarong and a black velvet cap, who had kept in the background, now made an approach. He was subdued and deferential.

"While they're at the market, I will show you the land."

"Good."

"It's high up, over the beach. Sandy. Very sandy."

"We can take the jeep."

"Good."

Totok relaxed and stepped back, as if he had been waiting for some time for the question of transport to the land to be resolved, while Haryati took note that he had completed his assignment successfully and offered cakes, urging people to eat.

"It's so late and we have so much to do tomorrow. So much."

She repeated the warning several times, making it sound like a criticism of her brother and his daughters for their late arrival.

"They had an accident, Ati."

"The roads are full of trucks these days."

"The plane was late."

Nevertheless, she continued to needle her brother, who eventually responded.

"This is the best meal we have ever had. Ti has done us proud this year."

Murmurs of assent and mild applause filled the room. Dutiful daughter number one clapped and prodded her sister. Haryati rearranged the dishes on the table, her eyes downcast, her lips open with pleasure.

After the meal, Mark was transported by a male relative to Pacitan's single motel, a short distance which might have been covered in silence had not Mark forced himself to remark on the excellent state of Pacitan's roads, compared with some of those they had travelled during the night. His companion listened, smiled and nodded, nodded and smiled, repeating the procedure at the motel before departing. Mark slept soundly. He was a seasoned traveller, so he did not feel entirely an outsider. His Indonesian was good enough to get the drift of conversation, and even to take part, while excluding himself from any exchanges that were quick or complex.

After a Dutch-style breakfast (eggs on fried bread sprinkled with hundreds and thousands), Mark was picked up by a group of women, including a bright-eyed Rukmini, and taken to the market. Auntie Ti led the way, bustling among the stalls, pointing and commenting on quality and price, aware of the presence in her little group of a foreign male and a noticeable young lady from Jakarta, but Rukmini made the decisions. She was paying. She bought a dozen chickens, not the biggest, nor the plumpest, but those with the shiniest feathers. The chickens were leg-tied, half-in, half-out of hessian bags under the feet of the stall holders, so her expedition through the chicken section created a commotion. The birds were decapitated at her nod. Having opened her purse, and closed it firmly, she stood back to allow others to carry the bloody purchases and moved on to the vegetables.

For Mark, Rukmini was like a princess among her people. They looked like any other gathering of Javanese – sturdily built, some faces thin and high-boned, some flat, round, snub nosed, none wearing hats, all dressed in the nondescript, loose and easily washable clothes that unwavering heat and bodily comfort dictated. She was dressed like everyone else in sarong and thongs, with a cotton shirt as a blouse, but she stood out because of her height, her pale skin and the poise of her head. Her hair was swept up, so that a clear view of the back of her neck balanced the tenderness of her face, even as she bought onions, carrots and cabbages with intense dedication in swift succession. And ten coconuts. Her entourage stuffed the purchases into an assortment of cardboard boxes and string bags.

"What about fish?" she asked.

The fish at the market was not worth buying, according to Haryati. The fresh fish were on the other side of town.

"They say it's the Australian surfers."

"What is?"

"They say the surfers are frightening the fish away."

Rukmini dropped back briefly to explain to Mark: "The people of Pacitan believe the Sea Goddess rules the Arafura Sea, right across to Australia. The Australian surfers who come here are too bold, riding the waves. The Sea Goddess might think they are defying her."

"Let's go to the other side, then," she informed her retinue. As there was only one car and nine overladen people, four returned to the house by foot.

"Ati, are you sure we have plenty of yellow rice?" Haryati was sure, although her "Yes" was dogmatic, sounding, with its flat assertiveness, as if it might have been uttered whatever the state of the supply of yellow rice, so Rukmini kept probing for real information. "How many this year?" "Between twenty and thirty." "Are you sure there's enough rice?" "Yes." "What about turmeric and galanga and lemongrass?" "Yes, enough."

Haryati's smile was patient and obedient, empty of any implication of amiability. The Pacitan clan was poor, proud and resentful and she was its mouthpiece. Keeping her head down in sullen acceptance, while continuing to watch her niece from the corner of her eye, gave her the appearance of discomfort as well as distrust.

"A batik shop in Bali has opened up here," she announced in the car, resuming some semblance of authority. "They say we'll be getting many tourists before long." Haryati paused in studied recollection. "Foreign tourists are the best. Their currency is hard."

Dutiful niece number two snorted. "Foreigners think they're marvellous."

"Prices will go up when the tourists come," said Auntie Ti. She was on uncertain ground, where foreign exchange rates and cultural prejudices were strewn like traps for the unwary, but on one subject she had the confidence of years of respected, if unsuccessful, advocacy. "It will be more expensive for us living here."

Rukmini heard, but paid no attention. They had reached the other market and she was scanning the benches of fish, some on ice under glass but most simply heaped in the open air. She chose, as always, by the sparkle in their eyes. "Dead eyes mean dead fish," said Aunt Ti approvingly. She suggested they should take the long way home, by the waterfront.

"They have gone to look at the land."

"What land?"

"I thought your father would have told you. We're looking at some land near the beach." She pointed in the direction of the sea. "Totok is thinking of building a motel."

"A motel!"

"For tourists. They like motels."

The other woman in the car giggled. "Why all that ...?" She was plump, enfolded in large quantities of cloth and as she giggled and flailed her arms, she sank, like a child in a heavily upholstered pram.

"What's funny?"

"Why all that ...?" The woman used the broken phrase again, as if it had proved to be useful. She threw her arms about in the air, simulating swimming. She put her head down and wriggled her neck, her arms outstretched, balancing each other. She was meant to be surfing. She released another well-used phrase. "Backpacks."

"There's no airport," observed Rukmini. "How will they get here?"

"Backpackers." Haryati was firm. "They like motels."

Rukmini took Mark's hand and remained quiet as the driver turned the car towards the sea. She always felt nervous when there was talk at the clan about change. Pacitan was for her old Indonesia, before independence, before the Dutch even, when the people were forced by isolation and shared poverty to live close to nature. She wanted them to stay that way and even when she admitted to herself that part of the reason was that she liked to play visiting princess from the outer space of Jakarta and Sydney, she also could not envisage her family in any other circumstance. If its members started adventuring, the family would disintegrate. The only way to keep them together was to keep alive the spirit that the clan had brought to Pacitan, in another century, from the medieval fastness of central Java. She was unsettled by this talk of buying land for a motel for tourists, who were only interested in cheap accommodation and would bring to Pacitan all the problems of Sydney's streets, drugs, freewheeling sex and a completely different view of the world.

The other woman in the car was still making a circling motion with her arms.

"Backpackers," Auntie Ti repeated. "They are not the usual kind of tourist. But their currency is hard." The other women examined her intently, so she added, "There's a book about them. You can buy it in Surabaya."

"Look, there they are."

Totok was standing with Haryo on a headland overlooking a curved beach and Rukmini made a quick decision to join them, asking Haryati and the woman to take the car back. "You had better get things moving at home. I won't be long."

Auntie Ti pouted. She wanted to hear the talk about the motel, but she said nothing. She had learned that if she wished to get her way it was not wise to argue, but if she pouted and stood still, there was a chance she would get what she wanted. But it was a stratagem that, while it worked with Totok, affected Rukmini only with contempt.

"The fish should not be left out in the heat," she said coldly.

Haryati's pout became a rueful smile of acceptance. She obeyed Rukmini not because she accepted her authority, but because she accepted the authority of her brother. She had learned from past encounters that when the issue was brought to a head Rukmini would be supported by her father, so she accepted during these short visits that she had to acknowledge the surrogate authority of her niece. Rukmini regarded this acceptance as her due, watching them leave with a stern countenance, as if, if she turned her back, Haryati could not be trusted.

Having exercised her authority, she was relaxed, turning to Mark with a smile. They climbed up the sandy cliff hand-in-hand, in full view of her father and male relatives.

"Remember Lake George!" he exclaimed.

She laughed, looked steadily at him. "This is no mountain."

"Maybe it is for me."

"What hidden meaning lies there!"

She slanted her almond-shaped eyes at him and there was an ironic edge to her voice. "Come on, don't be a weakling." She dropped his hand and ran. When she reached the top, however, she did not embrace the world as she had at Lake George, dancing in her tartan skirt and white stockings. She walked sedately to her father and stood by his side, looking calmly out to sea. In the distance, where waves were breaking, they could see the heads and arms of swimmers. Totok pointed.

"Packbacks."

When Mark reached the top, he felt a surge of wonder. He was an explorer who had come upon a postcard of nature. Perhaps it was the height, or the perfect curve of white sand, or the palms and she-oaks that moved lightly around him in the breeze, or the limitless sea, or just the contrast with the flat, plain township that straggled somewhere in the distance, but he felt light and airy. Tiny clouds moved overhead and he wondered if he could touch them. A thought came, like a thief in the night. He would build something here. It would pay homage to traditional Javanese architecture, somewhere between a fort, with high walls of stone and turrets of tufted grass, and a beach long house in a tropical garden. From its isolated, commanding presence, he and Rukmini would preside over the clan, guiding it, and the Indonesian nation, into new ways of thinking and behaving in a peaceful and prosperous world.

"Who?" asked Haryo.

"Australian tourists," said Totok. His smile was condescending, yet so tentative that it could be instantly disowned. "Swimming." He threw his arms about his head, put his head down and wriggled his neck, looking nervously at Mark. His laugh was a high-pitched tinkle that had come to him through generations of ancestors. As it was not his own, its purpose was obscure.

"How do they get here? There's no airport."

"By bus. Some have motorbikes." He spread his arms, wriggled his wrists. "Brrumm! Brrrummm!"

Haryo turned his back on the beach and looked at the land. It rose steeply from the water and was pitted with ravines, which were clogged with fallen and strangled trees. But on top it was flat and grassy. He stretched out his arms, measuring a chunk of the headland. It would take a good-sized building, with views all around.

"And all that's for sale?"

"Yes."

"You're sure?"

Haryo spoke as if the necessity to check information gained from Totok was accepted practice, after an embattled history of trial and error, not to be aired in public, but secure in family memory.

"Yes, Mas Yo. I've spoken to the owner." Pleased with his diligence, Totok waited calmly.

"Who is it?"

Totok was upset by the directness of the question. His face became pained and withdrawn, as if recording a sly assault on some part of his lower body. He shuffled his feet and wiped his hands on his hips. He stared out to sea.

"Dik To?"

He was not reassured by being addressed as a younger brother. He continued gazing out to sea. "Totok!" Shaken, he stepped forward and cupping a hand around one of Haryo's ears, whispered hurriedly. It sounded like "Tingalingaling".

"Who?"

Totok was reluctant to repeat the performance.

"Totok! It's not a secret, is it?"

"He doesn't live here."

Haryo sensed a complication. The name sounded Chinese. The people were sensitive about who owned land and although the authorities were not permitted to discriminate on grounds of race or religion, the clan's reputation (and his own) might suffer if it were thought that the vendor was Chinese. The transaction could still take place, but it might need to be managed through a third party.

"How did you speak to him then?"

"He was visiting."

"Oh, well." Haryo made his remark sound as if Totok's inability to be sensible and businesslike made the whole thing improbable.

"You could look at the papers," said Totok anxiously.

"Where are they?"

"They must be in Pacitan." Totok was uncertain. "Somewhere."

Haryo glanced at his watch. "The only time I've got is now."

Totok screwed up his face, acknowledging that the pressure of the present was one of life's unseemly necessities. Haryo looked at his brother-in-law impatiently.

"Well, come on."

They all descended carefully along a track cut into the headland by rushing water and someone with an axe. The jeep was parked on a dirt road at sea level. Haryo got into the seat next to the driver, speaking abruptly over his shoulder.

"What price is he asking?"

Totok seemed overwhelmed by the question, or perhaps by the answer that he was slowly preparing.

"Fifty." Furtively, he added, "Million."

"You're sure?"

Totok's throat was dry. He seemed unable to speak. He gripped the side of his seat and cleared the back of his throat.

"That's what he said."

"What's that?" shouted Haryo, as the jeep moved into a higher gear. "Can't hear you."

"That's what he said," croaked Totok. "He said ..." gathering his vocal chords together "... fifty million!"

"Fifty million," said Haryo softly. Rukmini whispered to Mark that it was a reasonable price. Prices were down because of the financial crisis. It was a good time to buy, if you wanted to build a motel for tourists, which she didn't. "Fifty million rupiahs is a lot of money," Haryo shouted, as the jeep lumbered from the hard, flat beach across tracks and wasteland to a bitumen road.

Number two daughter made a beeline for her father when they arrived at the house. "You've been looking at some land?" He nodded.

"Near the beach?"

"Yes. A good spot."

"For a motel?"

"Heavens, word gets around!"

"Motels are very fashionable. You don't have to register, or anything."

Haryo looked surprised. "You have to register, surely."

Rukmini rolled her eyes. "She means both of you don't have to register. One of you can stay in the car, while the other signs the register."

Haryo worried over the personal lives of his daughters. Since their mother's death, he had tried to act as their guardian, but had given up, handing over to Sumi, a loyal and good-hearted women who would do anything for the family but whose view of life combined earthy and moral attitudes that only she was able to reconcile. "They'll learn soon enough," she had said. While this was comforting as homespun wisdom, it did not meet Haryo's concern, which was with what they would learn. There was so much talk around, and not just talk but newspaper articles, about drugs and sexually transmitted diseases. Sumi's practical knowledge of how to keep young men at bay seemed alarmingly out of date. If he had had sons, he would have known what to tell them. He understood how men felt, how the sight of a woman's face, or perhaps the way her body moved, would set off a process of desire, the power of lust and the tenderness of love interacting with each other, sometimes one, then the other, more dominant, and he understood also how Indonesian society dealt with this primitive force, civilising it by recognising men's needs and protecting women from its harshest consequences. But he knew nothing of this new Western culture that everyone said was sweeping the country and which Muslim clerics he respected said was evil.

When Rukmini was still at school, she had had a romantic attachment to a young man who had died tragically. Since then she had seemed immune, either to liaisons or to marriage. He had tried to marry her to an army officer who came from a good family and had political connections, but she had refused, whether because he had tried to arrange the marriage, or because the boy was in the military, he did not know. He had merely mentioned the young man's name, placed him in her way, as it were; he had accepted that she needed to be attracted to him, for one reason or another, before they would marry. Still, she was very distant about it, not even bothering to respond, just waltzing off with that backward look she gave you when she wanted you to know she was leaving you behind. Now she had apparently married this middle-aged Australian with a lot of money. He did not know how serious she was about him (they had married in secret somewhere abroad, so legitimacy could be an issue), but bringing him to Pacitan for the annual ritual was significant. If she wanted a future in Indonesian politics (his secret wish) she should not be married to an Australian, no matter how wealthy. She should be living in Indonesia, married to an Indonesian. She spent so much time in other countries that she was in danger of losing touch with what people were thinking.

But he smiled to himself, as he always did when he was thinking of Rukmini. She was his accomplice in the great adventure of his life, the mission that never ended, the search for a way to unite the old Indonesia, with its fine thoughts and noble deeds, with the new Indonesia, with its lapsed faiths and fallen idols. Together, they connected the old and the new. It had always been like that and he was confident it would not change. Her sister was another matter. He did not see a political future for her. She was a practical woman who would prosper in business. She was always flirting and he suspected she did more than flirt. He did not know, however, and he did not know how to find out.

"These ... backpackers." He paused, as if the unfamiliarity of the word caused him pain. "What are they like?"

The two daughters adopted a ritual they had played since they were little girls. They raised their eyebrows, elevated their eyes to heaven, wriggled their bodies and lifted their arms, hands open upwards around their heads. The sister, who liked to undermine conversation with sweeping statements about life, responded.

"They're human."

"Of course, but ..."

"They're usually Australians."

"Well," Haryo reflected cautiously, "they're our neighbours." The putative son-in-law seemed to absorb the conversation without concern, although it was not clear how much he understood when, as now, they spoke in Bahasa.

"But not popular in Pacitan at the moment."

"These things come and go," said Rukmini.

"Students, mostly."

"Students have no money."

Haryo listened to his daughters, his head on one side. "No money. Nothing at all?"

"Well, nothing much."

"I was thinking of something simple for the motel," he said judiciously. "It is all we can afford."

"All *we* can afford?"

Rukmini gave her question a humorous twist and her sister drove it home.

"Guess who'll do the paying."

"Oh, well."

Haryo wiggled his head lightly from side to side, meaning that some of the world's ways were incorrigible. The daughters clapped each other's hands above their heads and waltzed off with backward smiles at their father. "Here we go again!"

The episode of the motel changed the atmosphere, which had for years been the same, calm and respectful, an acknowledgment of his role, even if administered by remote control from Jakarta, while he acknowledged in turn the importance of the clan's survival in Pacitan. The news that he was looking at land for a motel spread like fire, breaking out whenever more than a couple of people were gathered. He even overheard children chattering about it. No one was interested in the real purpose of the visit to the graveyards. He decided that he would need to give a "political" speech.

The men, all wearing black caps and dressed in plain shirts and sarongs in the traditional colours of deep blue and dark brown, gathered together in the front room of Haryati's house and were served a meal by the women. Mark sat with them, not taking part in the conversation, which he barely followed. He kept watching for Rukmini, but she did not appear. Her job was evidently in the kitchen, either preparing the meals or washing up. Her sister popped in and out, enjoying the male company. The meal was served in cardboard baskets and was not immediately eaten, the men smoking and talking. Then Haryo stood to deliver a short speech of welcome.

"Indonesia is going through difficult and challenging times," he said. "We must all band together to ensure that everyone in the clan is safe and sound. We must remember our history and our culture. We should not forget that we have survived other difficult and challenging times. We have survived because we have been united and because the clan's leadership has always stressed the importance of the group, not the individuals who are its members. There are many individuals, but there is only one clan. Of course, we must be progressive. You cannot stop progress. While we honour the past, we must look to the future because the future belongs to our children. But we must be sure that the future is right for our children. We do not want a future that will take them away from the clan. We do not want a future in which they will be forced to betray the very values that in the clan's struggle for survival we have learned to cherish."

He could see that the phrase "forced to betray" had hit its target. There was a murmur of agreement when he finished and some repeated the phrase. However, a mood of insubordination had taken over. They all wanted to go to the sea for the offering to the Sea Goddess, which was unusual. Other years, they had drifted off after they had been given the boxes of food. And this time, when they got to the beach, everyone was quiet, which was even more unusual. The few who went on previous occasions had made jokes about the Sea Goddess and had run in and out of the water like children pretending to be scared. This time, they stood around in small groups, their arms folded, as if they were surveying their domain. The small groups worried him. Were they beginning to form into factions, even perhaps cells? And this time none of the women came to the sea, which was also unusual. They clustered around Auntie Ti during the evening, and paid less attention to Rukmini. They had worked out that if a motel was built, those who lived in Pacitan, not in Jakarta, would run it. And, first, it had to be built, which meant that work would be available.

"So where will it be?" one of the men asked, at last.

"Where will what be?"

"The motel. Where is the land?"

"Oh, that." Haryo flicked a wrist, as if the subject were not worthy of notice.

The men mumbled among themselves, eyes downcast, but he was determined. He had decided that the subject of the motel had to be brought to a head and resolved. He knew that if his determination were made clear, no one would defy him.

"No motel," he said, with a slashing movement of one hand to give emphasis to the removal of the issue from the clan's agenda. And that was how it turned out, although the men showed their annoyance by not joining in the prayers when he cast an offering into the sea.

When Rukmini drove Mark to the motel that night and they made arrangements for an early morning departure, he wanted to show her that although he was aware, as she must also have been, that her father's failure to refer to their marriage was his way of implying that as far as the clan was concerned its existence was marginal, or even in doubt, he was pleased he had come and wanted to make light of the differences between himself and everyone else. "I don't feel at ease, sleeping comfortably in a motel while you're toughing it out in a cemetery," he said. Rukmini was terse. "Physically you're more comfortable, but emotionally I have the advantage." The subject was complex and personal and, in any case, it had been a long day and she had another topic in mind.

"What do you think of them ... the clan?"

"They seem pretty normal to me. The perpetual family topic ... real estate."

"They don't know what to do. They'd like everything to stay as it is, but this is a poor region. The soil is not good. There's no political leadership. If Indonesia was really a democracy, if they were part of some member of parliament's constituency, perhaps their voice would be heard. But they're ignored. They know they have to do something, but they don't have the money and the know-how."

She looked at him in the sideways manner she adopted if she wanted to try out something new and probably unacceptable.

"I sometimes think I should come back here and take over."

"I'd rather you stayed at the motel with me and took over."

Her laughter was automatic and short-lived and her parting smile was tentative and wan.

The visit to Pacitan changed Mark's view of Rukmini. She inhabited another world as well as his and she lived in that world with as much skill and authority, even more, as she did in his, and with much more than he could hope to live in her world. Australia had high living standards and good prospects, so it was expected that people would want to live there.

Every newcomer was a vote of confidence in the Australian success story. Indonesia, on the other hand, was densely populated and poor. It had absorbed waves of immigrants over the centuries, Hindu-Buddhist, Muslim and Christian, but its culture since independence was understandably in nationalistic mode, so that foreigners were not welcome. No matter how hard he tried, he would find it difficult to be accepted, except among a few of the business and professional elite.

Mark felt a pang of anxiety. But, as always, he slept well and at daybreak she reassured him, putting an arm around his waist as they walked to the jeep. Number two daughter grumbled sleepily, but Rukmini was as chirpy as a bird, giving no sign that she had spent the night consorting with foreign spirits or poring over the future of the clan with a depressed parent. He could not decide whether she was rejuvenated by her long-awaited night in the cemetery or relieved that it was over, the latter appealing to him when, climbing into the jeep, she announced, "I'll be glad to get home. Sleep in my own bed."

The driver had been hired for the expedition and did not understand why they had spent the night in a graveyard. He was irritable, because Haryo had said that he could not sleep on the back seat. He could curl up somehow in the two front bucket seats, if he wished, but not in the back. The driver did not know why Haryo had given him this instruction. He thought it must be to keep him alert, so he had stayed more or less awake all night, sitting up in the driver's seat, until Rukmini had appeared in the morning mist to tell him to pick up Mark at the motel. Actually, the reason was that Haryo did not want the impurities of the driver's body to affect the space where the girls would be sitting. It was important that for the first couple of hours of the return journey, when they turned their backs on Pacitan and faced the mists and mountains of central Java, they were undisturbed in the ambience of the ancestral presences and the associated thoughts that during the night he had impressed on them. Haryo barely noticed the driver's grumpy response. Every year, when he descended the hill from the tomb, even when he had stayed awake all night, he felt as if he walked on air. The aches and pains of ordinary life vanished.

The jeep climbed a winding road through sparse forest and small farms. The chalky soil was no good for rice paddies and the landscape seemed vacant. Haryo could see the coast, with a fringe of white surf between the green land and the blue sea and in his imagination Pacitan became a vast tourist resort. Foreigners swarmed over the hills, all wearing packs on their backs, some carrying surfboards like huge shields under their arms. Some were dressed in black, rubber tights and red helmets, like knights in armour. Some roared over the hills on motorbikes, blonde girls with bare legs and bouncing bosoms on their pillions.

He looked behind at his daughters, swaying and jiggling together, their faces serious, their eyes closed. The light of sunrise was behind them and the glow became an aura as he watched. It was a sign. His heart filled with happiness. The great adventure continued. "Go," he directed the driver, pointing north. "Go!" The driver grinned and put his foot on the accelerator. All was apparently forgiven.

"No motel," Haryo declared.

Mark had not been able to penetrate Haryo's manner of perpetual mystery. It was possible that he had for so long evaded giving a direct answer that he might not know any more how to formulate one, everything being for him so layered with different meanings that the only sensible course was not to disturb anything by referring to it directly. On issues of immediate interest, he would often remain silent, deferring to Rukmini. When he spoke about history, he would subside into adulation, as if these were characters in the drama so much larger than life, so much in the grip of forces beyond their control, or, if not, so captive of their own explosive personalities, that it was effrontery to treat them as normal human beings.

When they stopped for refreshments, Mark asked him about the prayers he offered at the tomb.

"These are the tombs of members of our clan who were among the first to come to Pacitan. They brought our family safely from the high turmoil of the Surakarta court to the peace of this lowly place. So I pray for guidance from them. I ask for the strength – and the wisdom – to discover ... the way ... forward." He added, as it occurred to him that his request might seem vague, "In these puzzling times."

He looked at Mark, no more than a wisp of a glance. "I ask for guidance for my two daughters, that they not be distracted from their purpose."

"How would you like to describe that purpose?"

Haryo turned away from his interrogator, as if the sight of him was too blatant communication. The question, Mark realised, was direct, although he had composed it carefully to avoid any suggestion of probe and pressure, so he felt obliged to apologise.

"I'm sorry if I seem to be prying, but you will appreciate, I'm sure, that this is something rare in everyday, practical Australia, so I am very interested in the way you associate your ancestors and your country's history with your daughters' future. The link."

"Not I," the father said. His face slightly turned, still not looking at Mark, he added, "I do not make the link. When we go to the graveyards, I ask in my prayers that the link be made."

It was a reprimand and the father now felt able to turn his face to his interrogator.

"Do Australians know they are tempting the Sea Goddess? Or is it just … ignorance of our culture?"

The question was more direct than Mark expected. He could not tell the father that Australians had never heard of the Sea Goddess, when the father's belief, which his dutiful daughter probably shared, was that the Sea Goddess would preside over any substantial relationship that might develop between Australia and Indonesia – and any serious relationship that might develop between an Indonesian woman and an Australian man. So he left uncontested the insatiable ignorance of the Australian people and he left unrevealed his intuition that if the Australian people were informed of the existence of the Sea Goddess and the powers attributed to her, they would laugh in the face of this ancient cultural myth.

Instead, he gave a brisk account of Australian exploration, how the forbidding hinterland had forced settlement on the coastal strip, how the combination of long, hot summers and the Christmas-New Year-National Day holiday season brought a concentration of family activity on the beaches, how the beach, exposing people to each other in … (virtually, and sometimes actually) … their birthday suits (choosing a phrase that would not offend) was a symbol of Australian democracy, how … He stopped. He was in need of the oblique response that the father had spent a lifetime perfecting.

Haryo nodded and reluctantly smiled.

Part Four

14

THE FINANCIAL CRISIS THAT DESCENDED on the tiger economies of Asia, like a judgment from the high priests of rationality, turned into a political crisis in Indonesia. Debt piled on debt fell like dominoes, assets subsided, foreign exchange rates collapsed. President Suharto resigned. Vice-president Habibie took over, pending elections, the first genuine political contest in the country for more than forty years. Also, there would be a referendum in East Timor, giving the people the choice of remaining as part of Indonesia or becoming independent.

Rukmini could barely contain herself. It was as if the dream of a lifetime, a dream she had thought would never become real, was suddenly as real as the potted roses she had brought to Mark's place from Sydney and were now lined up on the sunny side of the terrace garden. She met visitors at the front door before their finger had lifted from the bell button, her body in motion, her eyes searching for the latest news. She whirled them into chairs, darted backwards (a difficult feat she had perfected in her Sydney house) into the kitchen to turn on the hot water jug. She ran upstairs to check the fax machine, while continuing to converse in shouted bursts, and then ran downstairs (without touching the railing) to make tea and coffee with a clatter of cutlery, emerging, pink with exertion and delight, balancing a tray of mugs and a plate of biscuits.

From the moment the election was announced, she wanted to take part in it. From the moment the thought entered her mind, she began preparing, how to organise with friends in Jakarta a role in the campaign, how many suitcases to pack. She neglected her regular swim, she did not water the roses, her bed remained unmade each day until she tidied it before flopping into it at night. She spent hours on the telephone and her computer. And then, on one of her "deep pond" walks in the botanical gardens, she finally decided.

She saw from the corner of her eye a splash of blue. She hurried in the direction of her sighting and rounding a bend saw a jacaranda tree in bloom. She stood with her hands at her sides, in awe and delight. A flower dropped as she watched. The lawn under the tree was already a pink-purple carpet in the shape of the tree's foliage. She could not stop looking at it, but she also wanted to lose herself in it. She took off her shoes and tiptoed towards the tree, lying down under it, flat on her back, her legs and arms spreadeagled. The tree's ferny green leaves were just appearing. Its lizard-skin bark was dark in the sun. The tiny trumpet flowers were tenderly blue as they trembled against a pale sky and she closed her eyes tight to shut out the thought of how fragile, even frail, they were. It was so quiet she imagined she could hear the little flowers as they dropped.

It was not enough to say it was stunning. The fragile beauty of the jacaranda tree touched something deep inside her. She loved trees, but she always thought of them as strong, reaching down into the earth, up to the sky, withstanding heat and cold, wind and storm. Trees were part of nature's dark mystery and power. Yet here was a tree that produced a result as delicate as embroidery. In the jacaranda's poignant tenderness was a glimpse of another reality, which was that each kind of beauty was different, that diversity was life, and that in obedience to this law of nature, she had to create her own life.

In the kitchen that evening, she was suddenly still. She stopped chopping a carrot, quietly put down the knife and looked at Mark with tears in her eyes.

"I'm so lucky to have you."

She had been saying this, or something like it, for days and his response had a patina of preparation.

"Ditto."

"Yes, but ..." She would not be so generous with him. She would want reassurances from him that it was just political, that whatever the result of the election, nothing would change, that he would email or telephone every day, that she could visit him during the campaign and meet the people he was working with, that he would tell her immediately if he felt unwell or tired.

Mark interrupted, in his even-tempered, matter-of-fact Australian way. "If I were in your place I would do exactly the same, and you would agree, just as I am doing."

Her tears fell freely and he took her in his arms. Holding her, stroking her hair, he felt in some unfamiliar way to be under fire. He sought neutral ground.

"It's going to be hard work, but you've never been afraid of hard work. You will get caught up in the politics, but you've always been able to juggle what's public and what's personal."

She looked up at him through a veil of eyelashes and wet hair. "I would want you to tell me every day that you loved me. Twice a day!" She took up her knife and attacked the carrot. "But you just say yes. And that's it. You say yes and everything falls into place."

He kissed her nose, and then raised a clenched fist.

"Remember Lake George!"

"I could put an Australian opal ring through my belly button?"

"You could. But, why, for heaven's sake?"

"To show I'm yours."

"Should I wear batik underpants?"

"Yes." She was laughing with him but her eyes were serious. "You should!"

On a morning of scudding clouds and glistening sunbeams, Mark drove Rukmini to the airport. She was calm and detached, making light conversation about practical matters until they had to part. She turned to face him. They were experienced travellers, accustomed to farewells in airport departure lounges, but she wanted this to be different.

"I am so grateful to you for supporting me at this moment in my country's history. I thank you from the bottom of my soul."

"Go with the flow," he said. It was a phrase she often used with him, correcting his need for the logic of cause and effect. She laughed and kissed him lightly on the cheek. "I'm going to miss you terribly." As he watched her walk away, before she turned to wave and blow a kiss, he knew he would miss her differently from the many other times they had had to part. She was crossing the Arafura Sea to the dark mystery of Indonesian politics, poverty, passion and prejudice. He straightened his shoulders as he walked back to the car. She would manage; she always did.

The campaign was unlike any he had known. Opinion polls, policy platforms and pressure groups seemed not to exist, while political leaders wrangled among themselves as if the outcome of their manoeuvring would determine the result of the election and the fate of the nation. The election was for the parliament, which would then elect the president, but everyone, including the media, behaved as if it were a popular vote for the next president. Muslim leaders bickered among themselves on fine points of Islamic law and tradition, while they vied with Megawati Sukarnoputri, daughter of the first president and favoured to win, sometimes treating her as an ally against Golkar, the official government party that had ruled, in an electoral charade, for most of their lives, sometimes as a rival. Rukmini was working for a candidate close to Megawati and her ally, the Muslim cleric Abdurrahman Wahid, known affectionately as Gus Dur.

She kept in touch with Mark by e-mail, sometimes no more than a "Goodnight, darling, I'm exhausted", but often in graphic detail. Mysterious generals and colonels drifted in and out of her reports, actresses, singers, fashion models and other categories of pleasing women turned up unexpectedly, wishing to make their distinctive contribution, emissaries from sources unknown or unnamed came with money in brown paper bags, the former vice-president, now acting as president, although regarded as only a stopgap figure, summoned people, including other presidential candidates, for secret conversations. Rukmini was in the thick of it.

Gorgeous,

Total chaos, everyone going in different directions at the same time, phones constantly ringing and demands from every corner of the country. I am surprised how calm I am. When things go wrong I just apologise and keep going. I am known as "Ms Satpam" (satpam is the new name for the jaga, the night security man in expensive houses). I deal with the media and foreigners, especially the embassies. They are relieved to find someone who speaks English. I am trying to get our candidate to eat three meals a day, and take a siesta in the afternoon. He grabs food on the run and falls asleep at the most inconvenient times. I have also had a word with him about clothes. The country boy who looks after him personally has no idea what a political leader should wear. So our man, who has no idea either, is likely to turn up for a meeting with foreigners in a singlet and sarong. At a press conference he appeared in a purple shirt with pink flowers, which looked awful on television, especially as it didn't button up at the belly. I got some shirts like Nelson Mandela wears. And trousers that make him look as slim as possible (no easy task) and don't balloon like a clown's.

Must fly, Your loving wife, Rukmini.

He replied immediately.

Darling,

Thanks for the political pantomime. Never mind the candidate. How about you? Are you sleeping and eating well? The Australian media seems more interested in what is happening in East Timor than the Indonesian elections. Until now Timor has been overshadowed by Kosovo, but the killings in Liquica have been vividly reported. Is it possible to get someone to make a statement on East Timor? Stop the killings. Let us have all-Indonesia elections, then deal with East Timor's future?

I took out the daisies from the patch we made in the front garden. They weren't getting enough sun. I put in impatiens, the cherry-pink kind you see when you look out the kitchen window. Then I trimmed back the tree to let in more light. Then I cut down the fig tree! I stood on a step ladder and lopped off the top branches, then down and down, just like the professionals do. It wasn't as difficult as I expected. The wood cuts easily. Then I decided to do something about the kitchen cupboard. I bought some metal baskets that roll in and out. I am now in the process of trying to fit them in. Not easy. But I'm getting there.

It's beginning to turn to autumn, my favourite time, sunny, cool days. I miss not having you to share them.

Much love, Mark.

Then, when he was beginning to worry because he had not heard from her:

Scrumptious,

I haven't been able to turn around or even sleep, let alone write to you. Sumi died. It was awful. She had a stroke and was paralysed from the neck down. So Dad and I went to visit her. She lived in a small village at the border between east and central Java, Gombong, eight hours drive from Jakarta. So we left on Friday and arrived back on Saturday night. An emotional journey for me. When I saw her I just couldn't stop sobbing. She remembered me. She looked into my eyes and tried to signal something, but no words. Memories came flooding back, some painful but most of them beautiful. She was mother and friend to me. Then on Sunday, we left for Surabaya, Mojokerto, where my grandparents are, and Jombang. It was a reminder of the masses of poor people in Indonesia and how they are hoping that someone will bring them relief from their suffering. They wait for hours in the hot sun for our candidate. They form queues to kiss his hand. They come in hired trucks, buses, on bicycles, anything that moves. In a rally for Gus Dur in Mojokerto, two thousand jammed into a hall meant for two hundred. The place shook, the sound system died on us, and they just keep chanting "Whatever Gus Dur wants, we will do it for him" (it sounds better in Javanese). Then at Jombang something like sixty thousand people turned up at the town centre in a space about the size of a basketball field. The stage was three metres above the heads of the crowd and Gus Dur was like an entertainer. But not arrogant, like Western entertainers. On stage, he is like a child who doesn't know much about the world but wants to share his simple wisdom with everyone. He has a talent for dealing with serious matters by telling jokes. His party in Jombang is dominated by a group of fundamentalists, who try to spread the rumour that he is not a true Muslim, so he talked about tolerance. They listened in stunned silence while he translated Arabic love poems for them.

I love you to death.

Your loving wife, Rukmini.

She introduced him to the intricacies of campaigning in poor rural villages. Wahid's party, the PKB, was new and not well known. Many confused it with the more established Muslim party, the PPP. A jingle was invented: "Nine stars and number 35 is PKB." There were nine stars around a map of Indonesia on the PKB flag and PKB was 35 on the list of 48 parties in the campaign.

Gorgeous,

Mataram and Lombok one day, Banjarmasin the next, then Bogor and Bandung, Pasuruan and Langitan, then Palembang and Pontianak, followed by Ambon and Ujung Pandang. We are always way behind schedule because he keeps stopping to talk to people. I am full of admiration for his patience and humility. He doesn't rant and rave or promise the earth and there's none of that air-punching and hand-clasping that I dislike in Western politics. He just says he understands their suffering, that he will do what he can to help and they must be patient. He tells them that all human beings must respect each other's beliefs and that racial prejudice is immoral, because people have no say in who their parents are. He tells jokes, often a bit salty. After each joke there is a quiet second or two, as people turn it over. Then there is a murmur of appreciation and a movement of heads, no laughter. It's so different from Western elections. It's more like a prayer meeting.

Hugs and kisses, Your loving wife, Rukmini.

She always signed off as "Your loving wife", no matter how short or long the letter.

A crinkled brown paper parcel arrived, either hurriedly dispatched or handled by an inquisitive official, bearing a cluster of Indonesian stamps as colourful as the chest of an army general. Inside was a pink and green map (with blue water) of Jakarta, so large (one metre by two metres, on a scale of one to 20,000) that it could only be appreciated if spread on the floor. It was on smooth paper, as if it had been waxed, intended to be unfolded section by section and read in wind and rain, and then to be folded and thrust into cavernous pockets of trousers worn by marauding soldiers and bush walkers. Mark unravelled it on the floor, examining it from time to time in the hope that its purpose would be revealed, but its size and detail were so far beyond the needs of anyone not contemplating bombing Jakarta or spending a week driving and walking through it, that he could not penetrate its mystery. If it had been a map of the entire country, it would have been useful as a guide to the election campaign but it covered only Jakarta and, in any case, did not show electoral boundaries. Impassive and mysterious, it remained spread out on the floor.

Handsome,

I have noticed that the cameras have lately begun to turn my way, because of gossip about me and our candidate. The question has been asked by some of the evangelical Muslims why I have been allowed to stand near him when he is speaking. I have made no public comment, but I have told some media friends that we are cousins and that, as family, it is alright for me to be near him. The yellow press (aided and abetted by our political rivals) is hinting that I am his second wife. If any of this rubbish reaches Australia, just ignore it. I carry your picture with me and it's the first thing on my desk. My gay hairdresser thinks you are handsome and has offered to show you the sights of Jakarta. "He's mine," I said, "and don't think you can get him by messing up my hair!" Speaking of clothes, I've had a couple of slacks made with long shirt tops. It's the modern Islamic gear. Just to make sure I can't be criticised for being too Western, I've bought some scarves to throw over my head. You will be surprised how demure I look.

Your loving wife, Rukmini.

In a stifled attack of jealousy, Mark telephoned. She was surprised, thinking it must be bad news, and then pleased. "I'm glad you rang. Did you get the map?"

She explained that her father had become reconciled to their marriage. He had placed a photograph of them together in his living room, for all to see. He had agreed that they could build a house on his block of land in Jakarta. Alternatively, he had found land at Puncak, a hill resort outside Jakarta. An architect friend was drawing up plans for a house (five bedrooms, for a growing family!) that could go on either site. She preferred her father's block and she had sent the map so that he could see where it was, not close to the main city but near a freeway. She gave him the address and the site on the map, and he did not get to inquire about the veiled headdress and the imaginary relative because she overwhelmed him with the news that as soon as the elections were over she would return to Australia and, depending on the result, they could make plans. All the indicators were that her side, the anti-government coalition, uneasy but holding, would do well.

"Some sceptics here are saying that the elections will never be held," he said.

"The same here," she said. "But we think they will. Perhaps polling day will be postponed a bit. The machinery isn't ready, and some in the government are not used to having a real contest. But we're too far down the track to turn back."

Their conversation was businesslike, without the soft words of fun and affection they liked to exchange. She sounded busy, and others were probably present. He chided her mildly for not responding to questions he had asked earlier on urgent money matters. Next morning, a dozen red roses were delivered, with the note, "Sorry. I love you very much."

Sweetheart,

Aceh was a shemozzle. We underestimated the real anger against Jakarta and the Javanese. We were supposed to meet students in the early afternoon then the masses at the stadium nearby. At the student hall a violent demonstration became ugly. Getting him into the hall was a mistake, posing a physical threat not just to him but to all of us with him. Getting him out was a miracle. I have tried to get bodyguards but it is expensive to take them with you everywhere. But after Aceh I've threatened to do some fundraising for them myself. Actually, it turned out well in the end. The student leaders came to our hotel in the evening and apologised. We had a very frank and open discussion. One student told us how his mother had been raped before his eyes, another how his father was butchered to death. They just want the military out of their lives. There is a real campaign in Aceh against the elections. People have been killed by snipers. Our man was his loving self, listening to them and saying he understood their suffering. He is preparing a report to the military leadership in Jakarta based on what the students told him. I am exhausted and must get some sleep for an early morning.

Security problems were eventually resolved by the appearance of what Rukmini called "Dad's army – except that there are 250,000 of them". They were the Ansor boys, a volunteer youth group of the big Muslim organisation Nahdatul Ulama, except that they were not boys but men of all ages. They wore green uniforms with white stripes and many of them rode motorcycles. Six of them were assigned to her, walking behind her in file and occasionally inquiring if she was too hot. She described the effect on one visit.

We had to claw past the trucks and traffic jams, no security in sight, then a scattering appear and try to make way for us, but the traffic gets worse, we are stuck behind a huge lorry, with the boys on bikes and pick-up trucks way ahead of us. Then suddenly hundreds of them on motorbikes come riding in the opposite direction. I mean hundreds. They all do a U-turn at the same time and it becomes a nightmare. We are in a huge traffic jam, with hundreds of men shouting "Gus Dur" and hundreds of drivers cursing them. The police take fright and two cars panic, taking to the verge with sirens wailing and blue lights flashing. I wished you were here. I couldn't stop laughing. If only Gus Dur could see properly.

࿇

On his way back from a business trip to Singapore, Mark was able to meet Rukmini briefly in Jakarta. She took him, with her father, to the house of friends, the woman from primary school, the man successful because of some favoured position he had managed in relation to oil concessions. Behind the discreet, tightly guarded front of the house in Menteng, the rooms opened up like an Oriental palace, flowing into each other around an ornamental fountain, a pink enclosure of sofas and piled cushions, a gallery of dark wood cabinets and mirrors edged in black, a swimming pool of limpid blue tiles, a television room with a screen as large as the back of a delivery van. The guest of honour was not her, nor indeed Mark, but a colonel who had married one of the president's daughters and was therefore more than a simple soldier. Also present was the manager of a weekly magazine, a couple who had a catering business and a Muslim poet, much admired for his Arabic translations. The colonel was late, detained at the palace.

"He's always being detained at the palace," said their host. He was lean, angular, adventurous. He and the colonel rode trail bikes together when they were abroad. Indonesia was too crowded.

The guest arrived with a clatter of activity at the front door – a motorcade, shouted orders, the sound and smell of metal and leather, a head peering around the door, and then a handsome, smiling man wearing an orange beret, which he removed and handed to an orderly as he entered. Almost immediately, as he and his host exchanged pleasantries, each with a hand on the other's shoulder, his mobile rang and he swung away, clamping the piece to his ear, turning his back to incubate the conversation. It was short, but apparently had import. His boyish face was troubled when he turned to his host, and they retired immediately to a side room.

"Let's eat," said their hostess. "They could be there all day."

It became apparent that the purpose of the lunch was to give the colonel an opportunity to air his views, which, in his absence, left a vacuum which none of those attending had been chosen to fill. Whether this was a special occasion or whether at luncheons the colonel attended it was always like this was not clear, at least to Mark. He suspected that Rukmini might know, but he was content to go along with events as they unfolded. He was still coping with the fact that from the moment she had met him at the airport, he had sensed that Rukmini was different. For a start, her hair was cut very short, replacing what she had called (with affectionate contempt) her "flowing locks" with a businesslike bob. Also she was nervous, as you might expect of someone involved in many, simultaneous activities over which she had no control but (to a degree he could not assess with confidence) had some responsibility for. Her movements had always been quick, but always with a smile and a commanding tilt of her head. Now, she seemed startled and anxious.

Their hostess was more timid than other of her school friends he had met and their host was more overbearing. Their wealth was not her style, nor the style of other Javanese he had met through her. She did not join in the conversation or did so carefully, not in her usual splatter-gun fashion.

The lunch proceeded in fits and starts. It was in the style of Indonesian meals, which were presented as sumptuous feasts, and the procedure was not to sit down at table but to line up to fill your plate from platters of food laid out on the table, and to retire to a chair or couch, balance plate and napkin on your knees and hope for the best – that you didn't spill food on your lap or the floor, which was spread with Persian carpets. Conversation rarely flowed until eating was over, a convention that in this case was doubly true. Even when the two men emerged, they served themselves and sat apart, in earnest conversation.

Eventually, the centre of attention acknowledged his social duty, and after the host's introduction set about providing the guests with an insight into deeper layers of influential thinking at the palace than could be exposed in official statements or had managed to find expression in the media. Refreshed with a whisky and soda, he did this by taking strong and controversial positions which everyone assumed must have some kind of credibility at the palace. The Asian financial crisis had hit Indonesia badly. Jakarta was being pressed by Western governments to accept loans and policy advice from the International Monetary Fund.

The colonel's handsome, boyish face was so lively and personable that it was hard to pay attention to what he was saying. When he smiled, which he did often, it was as if he were responding to a personal compliment, rather than to the content of what he had said. It became apparent after a while, however, that his message was an intolerant mix of satisfaction, provoking spasms of overbearing confidence, and disapproval, implying deep anxieties.

"The president has frequently spoken of the three don'ts. 'Don't be easily surprised, don't be overwhelmed by anything, and don't overestimate your own position.'"

While they mulled over this inescapably sensible advice, the colonel took several calls on his mobile telephone, barking out instructions. Free at last to resume his lecture, he picked it up to his own liking. "There is a conspiracy against Indonesia by Western governments and Western media. What is wrong with Indonesia?" He patrolled the room, asking the ceiling the question with outstretched hands. "What is wrong with Indonesia?" Then he turned to his little audience and gave it his solemn answer.

"It is a Muslim country and its military is politically powerful. So anything it does is wrong." He extended one hand and ticked off a succession of fingers. "Whether it's East Timor or West Irian. Or giving Indonesians control of the economy. Or blocking foreign ideas like freedom of the media. Or ..." He flourished a tabulated hand; the possibilities were endless.

The Indonesian journalist had been drinking and was in a belligerent mood. "Why don't we tell them to go to hell, like Sukarno did." The colonel nodded his encouragement.

"Actually Indonesia is treated sympathetically by Western governments."

Mark had not intended to speak and surprised himself. His intervention, contrastingly cool and level, shocked the colonel into silence, and to fill a vacuum that he thought might be embarrassing to Rukmini, Mark quickly added: "I agree the Australian press, and probably the Western media in general, can be critical at times, but that's because it's in their nature. Finding fault in others, while ignoring their own, is their way of life. The Australian media treats Australian politicians in general, and any incumbent government in particular, as if they are only in politics to look after themselves. Well, I have some sympathy with a healthy scepticism. And, I imagine, there are faults even in Indonesian governments." He caught Rukmini's eye. "The Australian government, however, has been understanding and well disposed to Jakarta."

The colonel observed Mark with indifference, as if from a distance. "Perhaps you are not aware of recent developments. Not in the loop." He liked the phrase and repeated it. "Not in the loop."

He raised his hand again. "Chinese money leaving the country." Tick. "Israeli and Singapore intelligence working together." Tick. "Look at all the Jews around the White House ... Albright, Berger, Cohen, Rubin, Reich." Tick. He had run out of fingers and now held both hands aloft. "Greenspan running the Federal Reserve, Wolfensohn running the World Bank." His wholesome good looks barely faltered as he listed the names of the conspirators.

Mark thought to himself that only the most simple-minded or fanatical could undertake such dangerous leaps in logic but he felt constrained as an outsider not to intervene. Haryo sat with eyes downcast and Rukmini was quiet. Even the talkative journalist was subdued. The colonel dominated conversation so completely that it became a monologue, increasingly erratic and obsessive. The colonel drove home his point over and over again. It was no fault of the Indonesian president and his family and no fault of the Indonesian government, especially its military component, and no fault of the Indonesian people that the country was in such a mess. It was the fault of the world outside, which did not understand the Indonesian way of doing things.

The poet famous for his Arabic translations had been completely silent. Suddenly he stood, a dramatic sight in belted gown with epaulettes, and recited:

Tak ada lagi bumerang
Tak ada lagi tombak;
Kini kita sudah berbudaya –
Diskriminasi dan bir.
Tak ada lagi tarian,
Yang riang dan hura-hura.
Kini kita punya bioskop
Kalau nonton bayar saja.
Tak lagi berbagi
Hasil buruan ini.
Kini kerja untuk uang,
Ludes untuk memborong barang.

The guests ventured mild laughter and nods of approval.

Dulu telanjang saja
Tak pernah malu rasanya;
Kini kita berpakaian
Menyembunyikan anunya.

This brought roars of laughter, so he translated for Mark's benefit.

No more boomerang
No more spear;
Now all civilised –
Colour bar and beer.
No more corroboree,
Gay dance and din.
Now we got movies,
And pay to go in.
No more sharing
What the hunter brings.
Now we work for money,
Then pay it back for things.
One time naked,
Who never knew shame;
Now we put clothes on
To hide whatsaname

And, with concluding bravado:

Lay down the woomera,
Lay down the waddy.
Now we got atom bomb
End everybody.

A successful performer, he bowed to applause, then identified the author, Australian Aboriginal poet Oodgeroo Noonuccal. It was a nice touch that might have produced a convivial interlude. How did an Indonesian specialist in Arabic poetry become interested in Australian poetry, especially Indigenous poetry? But mention of the atom bomb had ignited the colonel.

"India and China have the bomb, why not Indonesia? Pakistan has it. Israel has it and someone in the Middle East will soon get it to equal Israel, and then compete with Pakistan to represent the true voice of Islam. Indonesia is the largest Muslim country in the world. Why should we not have the bomb?"

He appealed to each member of his audience, as if they were personally denying Indonesia the bomb. There was a concerted campaign in the West to keep Indonesia down. "Down boy!" he exclaimed. It was not clear whether he was suppressing a dog or a coolie. But he was clear on one point, which he repeated again and again. It was not the fault of the Indonesian government. It was the fault of the Americans, the overseas Chinese and the Israelis, all of whom were in the grip of commercial greed, unable to understand the Indonesian way of doing things.

"Food and clothing for the people, that's the Indonesian way, not budgets and balance of payments and ..." The colonel trailed a hand airily in conclusion.

Haryo rose to his feet, a slight figure. "There is a limit to the amount of learning a human being can absorb on any single occasion." He spoke in English, bowing graciously to host and hostess, and then nodding to Rukmini and Mark. "My party is leaving."

He departed, ignoring the colonel and the poet, Rukmini and Mark in his wake. An unnatural silence on the drive to Haryo's house was broken by Mark, from the back seat.

"You put the colonel in his place very elegantly."

The father stared ahead. "The poet made fun of us."

Rukmini, who was driving, explained that an Indonesian expert on Arabic poetry who translated Aboriginal verse obviously did not take ancient Indonesian culture seriously. Mark considered the possibility that the father had walked out on the poet, not the colonel.

When they reached Haryo's house, Mark opened the car door for his father-in-law and formally shook his hand. "It has been important for me to be with you and your daughter at this moment in Indonesia's history." Haryo nodded and departed. "Good luck in business," he said over his shoulder, waving a languid goodbye.

Rukmini was silent on the way to the hotel where Mark would stay before taking an early morning flight to Australia. She could not stay with him at the hotel; she had to hurry to the airport to join a group travelling to Banjarmasin in Kalimantan for a political rally. He sensed that she was struggling to reconcile layers of feeling deeper than conventional politics and history.

"The colonel was a bit hard to take," he offered.

"He'll probably be president one day. He's got the right connections." She sounded wistful. "Dad wants me to be serious about politics. He thinks I'm Indonesia's Aung San Suu Kyi." She glanced sideways in a mocking manner. "He thinks he's the father of the true Indonesia."

Mark smiled. "I've been getting that impression."

"What he doesn't realise," said Rukmini, briskly, "is that the army will never let Suu Kyi run the country." She repeated her mocking, sideways look, followed this time by a burst of laughter. "She's married to an Englishman."

He stood at the window of the hotel room. Opposite was a huge, anonymously internationalist new hotel, in which one of the president's children had an interest. On its steps were prostitutes as young as schoolgirls, and other ragged signs of Indonesia's underclass, bedraggled beggars and transvestites, with their fragile, lilting voices. At the centre of the traffic circle was one of those Sukarnoist statues of the nationalist era, heroic Indonesian figures welcoming the dawn of a new era, which had been scorned as Stalinist propaganda by the Western media. Now its bold outline seemed heroic. In ceaseless flow around it were the signs of Indonesia's new wealth, sleek new cars with shaded windows of bulletproof glass, fleets of motorcycles. And he was standing at the window of a hotel he liked for its elegant, understated, interior feeling and the fact that it made no effort to disguise its Chineseness.

"Indonesia's like Australia," he said, turning to her with a sudden burst of cheerfulness. "A work in progress." She came over to him, the tip of her nose pink from the scrubbing she had just given her face in the bathroom, and hugged him, nestling against him with a huge sigh, whether of pleasure, relief, admiration, affection, or all of these, he was uncertain.

"I don't know what I'd do without you. I never thought I would have enough stamina for politics."

"So it's all due to me?"

"Yes, darling." She altered her tone of voice, becoming teasing. "It's all your fault."

"The way the world is going, being Australian or being Indonesian is going to be a thing of the past." He was speaking over her nestled head, beyond her.

"But our children will be Australian," her muffled voice protested. She pushed him away and spoke clearly. "They will have to live somewhere while they're growing up."

She liked to embarrass him with simple truths. It was as if she were trying to force his thoughts to the surface, where she could see them. He was reserved, thoughtful, serious, even intense, rarely exposing his feelings. Very Javanese, in fact. She was direct, active, pragmatic. Very Australian. And she seemed determined that night to be unambiguously Australian.

"You're part of the global elite," she said. "Business skills and the English language."

He pretended to be puzzled. "And you?"

"Part of the global mass, struggling to keep its head above poverty."

"You're an aristocrat, like your father," Mark said. "Ruler of Indonesia's destiny. And I'm a democrat, ruled by the ballot box and the market."

"And we're both part of the ... global thingo?" She gave a little laugh of embarrassment. "You say it."

"The secular, humanist, democratic, transparent new world order."

They looked at each other and burst into laughter.

"I love the way you say it," she said.

15

When polling day came, Rukmini attended with her father. She e-mailed Mark:

I cannot tell you how proud I feel today. I am actually voting, for the first time in my life, in a real Indonesian election. The people have lined up in the hot sun for hours, waiting their turn. I thank you from the bottom of my heart for letting me have this opportunity.

During the long wait, as every vote was checked and counter-checked to prevent fraud, a rumour surfaced that the computer operators who were keying in the results had been bribed by the government. Substantial amounts of International Monetary Fund money, intended for the recovery of the Indonesian economy, had disappeared. Each ballot paper had to be checked again by hand. At each daily count, her side, the opposition, emerged on top, not enough to secure a majority by itself, but the largest slice of the vote. Now these votes would be translated into seats in the body constitutionally empowered to elect the president. Then the dealing would begin.

The people have had their say, now the elites decide. The horsetrading begins. There will be deals about big contracts. There will be deals with the military about jobs in the state enterprises and how much (e.g. oil) revenue they can have. And whether they should go back to barracks. I am suddenly exhausted. I can't wait to get back to simple things, my kitchen and garden. And my bath of perfumed oil. And you. I am missing you. Prepare, lover boy. After pungent male odours (campaigning Indonesian style is very basic), I can't wait to smell your sweet flesh. In fact, I can't wait to touch it. Get strong, handsome, prepare to be assaulted!

She gave a blow-by-blow account of the negotiations, in ancestral tombs in the dead of night, in smoke-filled hotel rooms, on golf courses. She recounted in detail the failure of the friendship between Gus Dur and Megawati to overcome resistance among Muslims to a female president. Then came the news. Gus Dur was president.

Mark prepared for Rukmini's return. He ordered flowers, had her car tuned, rearranged her pots, leaving the roses for her to prune, got in a load of firewood. He sorted her clothes; she had left in autumn, been away all winter and now spring was coming. It would be a celebration, but it would also be a time for reflection. They would need quality time together. Big decisions would have to be made.

While she was away, he had reorganised his financial assets. The transport business was too cumbersome to be run efficiently by someone who was never there. You needed to be there, hands on. If he was going to be dividing his time between Indonesia and Australia, he needed to make some senior appointments and become more entrepreneurial himself. The global economy that created more competition in the transport business also created opportunities. Patricia, with the gleaming teeth, urged him to take stock. "There's stormy seas ahead," she said, with the corners of her mouth down.

Mark would say later that his life could be divided into before and after the e-mail from Rukmini that arrived the day before she returned. At first, he thought it was a joke which, possibly because she was tired and unable to think in English, she had not managed to bring off.

Dear Mark,

This must be the hardest letter I have written in my life. I have had a deeply spiritual experience. I would not be writing this letter if it were not serious.

I did not go looking for this to happen. I arrived in Indonesia committed to our marriage. There was no plan to scheme or cheat on you. All this has happened so naturally and fast. I have never felt like this before. It is powerful and has touched the core of my being. I now feel closer to God and so much more comforted in the spiritual sense. I feel I have finally arrived home.

I don't know what else to say except that I have to be honest with you. I am not going to pretend behind your back and lie to you. The truth is there is not much to say except that it has happened and that I now want to live in Indonesia, have a Muslim marriage and Muslim children. I am sorry to have disappointed you. I know you were looking forward to me coming back. This letter has ruined it. I am myself stunned by this development and can only apologise to you. All this has been so much larger and more powerful than myself.

Take care, Rukmini.

P.S. I am still coming back to Melbourne as planned.

He printed the letter and read it again, hoping that on paper its message would become clear or perhaps nonsensical. He took his morning coffee to a small opium table he had bought in Hong Kong, from where he could see through a glass wall her roses, lined up to catch the sun. He read the letter again. Cheat on you. Muslim marriage. Muslim children. Arrived home. Disappointed. Ruined. Stunned. Apologise. He sat and looked at her roses, his mind empty and whirling. It was impossible! Yet her letter was pointed and purposeful, as if everything were settled. It was not a joke. She was deadly serious.

But what exactly had happened? She had had a religious experience, which apparently meant that their marriage was over. The steps in between were Muslim marriage and Muslim children. There was no mention of a Muslim father, although she was assuming (reasonably enough) that it would not be him. The style of the letter puzzled him. It did not have the desperate edge he would have expected – the scattergun justification, the defence of herself by counterattack, the erratic sidesteps in logic that she always claimed showed that while her mind might not be strong, her

155

conscience was clear. It was calm and determined, almost pre-determined, as if her hand had been guided by a different person, herself but profoundly changed, or even, perhaps, by another.

The letter contained two Rukmini-isms, "cheat on you" and the frank admission that it would "ruin" the anticipated pleasure of her return, each of which, as he reread the letter many times, lost their clumsy charm and became chilling; they had the ring of authenticity. This was a controlled and careful letter, all the more because its ominous tone was at odds with its content. If what she was talking about was some kind of religious conversion, she was quick to project from it the end of their marriage. She did not ask for understanding, which he would readily have offered, although he could not take her references to God seriously. He took them to indicate her elevated feelings: she had always been spiritual, not religious. She had scorned her mother's faith and had been scathing of Muslims who wanted to turn Indonesia into an Islamic state.

Was it possible the letter had been written by someone else? No, she would never allow that. But it was not her usual style. And why was she coming to Melbourne? As a gesture? To collect her things? In order to negotiate some kind of settlement? To make legal arrangements?

On the drive to the airport, he tried to get his thoughts in order. His throat was still dry and his stomach still ached, but his mind moved beyond the bleak message of her letter – "I feel I have finally arrived home." He brushed it aside, but it returned. Her phrasing – it sounded like her – was convincing, because of its suggestion that she had been on a long journey, and now wanted to stop. The issue of identity had been present as long as he had known her. Her ancestors were alive in her memory. They had been fighting the Dutch before the Australian nation existed. When they had toured the world together, he had sensed at times another world: battles fought long ago between warriors under flags that still brought a shiver of pride.

He drove into the wrong parking area, a spiral ascent into No Parking and No Entry signs that were part of the redevelopment of a seemingly interminable airport terminal. By the time he reached the section for international arrivals, she was already there, waiting with her trolley.

She stood still, steadily watching him approach. She had lost her darting eyes and a body in perpetual motion. When he reached her and before he could touch her, she handed him a bottle of duty-free gin, his preferred purchase on international flights. He had brought her blue coat, knowing that she would be cold, and she turned her back to put it on. Then she grasped the handle of the trolley and, eyes downcast, pushed her luggage towards the car park, like a careworn shopper.

"I'll do it." Mark was pleased to find an opportunity to intervene.

She surrendered the trolley and they did not speak until they reached the ticket machine. It had been her prerogative to operate ticket machines at airport car parks, a mark of her familiarity with the latest technology that he did not have, nor need. He waited with the trolley while she stood in line. When her turn came, she solemnly confronted the machine and extracted the necessary responses without her usual grunts of recognition as it performed to her satisfaction. They took a crowded lift to the level where the car was parked. As they left the lift and moved towards the car, he broke the silence.

"Well, you've certainly given us something to talk about."

She stopped in her tracks. "I want a divorce."

He was so surprised that he could not assemble a response, yet the shock of what she had said was lost in the shock of how she looked. Admittedly, the midnight from Jakarta was no fun run and she would have been dreading this moment. But her strident voice and the hostility in her eyes were all so new to him that she was another person. An image from an old American film flicked into life: a peroxide blonde who had wheedled her way into the affection of an industrial tycoon announced, legs apart and finger pointed accusingly at her erstwhile benefactor, "I wanna deevorrrce."

He turned away, pushing the trolley towards the car, playing for time and sanity. She followed, repeating, "Do you understand? A divorce." People stopped pushing trolleys, loading cars and exchanging gossip to watch. He stopped the trolley until she came closer. He spoke to her softly.

"This isn't the time or place."

"It's my human right!"

They were standing in the middle of a traffic lane, she shouting, he unable to look her in the eye.

"Alright." Her mind was racing, in top gear. "Then it's over to the lawyers."

She strode ahead, looking for the car. He trundled behind in a state of bewilderment. She greeted him with flashing eyes, standing at the driver's door. "It's my car. Give me the keys."

It was indeed her car. He had thought she would be pleased to see her little white sedan again. He gave her the keys and she briskly started the engine while he was still loading her luggage. They began a long, silent drive home. Occasionally he glanced sideways at her profile, hoping that she would perhaps turn to him, saying, "Why are you looking at me like that?" In the deadly silence, sitting close together, as they had so often done while she produced the scenery and he expounded on the reason why effect should follow cause, not the other way around, he convinced himself that she would suddenly turn to him, saying, "I'm sorry, darling. I feel like mashed potatoes. I didn't sleep on the flight, worrying about this." But she did not turn to him. Or say anything. Her eyes were fixed on the road, and on some cold and distant star.

Yellow and red rods, looking like huge pencils, had been erected on the freeway as a striking entrance to the city, suggesting a welcome arch to those with imagination. The angled shafts startled newcomers and amused Melburnians. It occurred to him that this unexpected and conspicuous welcome might distract her. If he could think of something to say about post-modernist Melbourne, she might give him one of those slanted smiles that would mean all was not lost. He remembered a distant Sunday school phrase that had stayed with him, "neither immanent nor transcendent". Then, reminded of her new religious disposition, he became alarmed at her likely response and while he fumbled, she drove through the arch without so much as a raised eyebrow.

Over the next few days, as he went through the routine of living in his house with someone whose mind was elsewhere, he could feel what was happening on two levels. At a personal level, he was torn, unable to believe that this withdrawn and ominous presence was the delicious person who had been his adored and adoring companion, who had taught him about love and loyalty, even after death, and for whose honesty he would have sworn in the highest tribunal of any land, whatever its culture. Whether she had already betrayed, or merely wished to betray, their marriage was still unclear to him, but she certainly seemed determined to destroy everything else that had been precious to him.

At another level, as he stared into the darkness, sleepless in bed, he could see clearly and precisely what was happening, but he would not allow himself to be convinced because if it were true, the person who he thought had discovered the secret of life was nothing more than a ruthless politician. She had, he admitted, a nose for the main chance. With her usual enthusiasm, she had thrown herself into Indonesian politics and at an exciting moment her life and her country's history had come together, so that she would not easily have distinguished one from the other. He could understand how, in the fever of election campaigning, she had convinced herself that this was a new phase in her life. Now that the election had brought people she knew to power, she had the chance of a lifetime. There was much to be done in a country as poor as Indonesia. She was needed, could make a difference and with friends in high places, could be given the opportunity.

Was it not possible she had decided to reinvent herself for the purposes of a new career? Was it not possible she had decided to sacrifice him because he was no longer an asset? With Australia pushing for East Timor's independence and with Muslim vigilantes active in democratic Indonesia, being married to an Australian infidel was a liability. But was she so hard-hearted that she could discard him with a slap from the back of her hand? Or was the brutality a façade, because she could not trust herself to be open and honest with him?

For three days, he tried to begin a conversation, but she would say only that she had had a deeply religious experience, repeating like a litany what she had written: she was a different person now, closer to God than she had ever been, and she wanted to become a Muslim, make the obligatory visit to Mecca, have a Muslim marriage and Muslim children. She recited her "rights" and her "interests", as if they were negotiating a diplomatic agreement; by protecting her rights she was looking after her interests. It was not in her interest to tell him in detail what had happened or to explain, apologise or disclose her future plans.

During the day, she went out for long periods. In the evenings, she retired to her bedroom, telephoned Jakarta and read the Koran. Her manner was insensitive to the point of rudeness, so unlike her; even when angry, she was always polite about small things. Her withdrawal carried with it a studied disapproval, as if the emotional turmoil in which they found themselves was his fault, as if she were the wronged party, entitled to have her nose in the air. Sometimes she said it.

"I'm doing you a favour by being here."

He hit back. "You wreck our lives, then say you're doing me a favour by coming back to survey the damage."

"I came back to talk it over."

"Then why aren't we talking it over?"

"I've told you all there is to tell. It's happened. That's all there is to it."

"Then why the hell did you bother coming back?"

She shrugged her shoulders. At that moment, Mark thought he might never have known Rukmini. Take away her warm and lively presence, remove his confidence that she loved him and that therefore everything she said or did was in his favour and, suddenly, she was unpredictable, an uncertain quantity, even a hostile force. Perhaps their life together had been so effortless that they had not had to face that part of each other that was hidden, the stuff of dreams and desires, anxieties and prejudices. He had trusted her completely and she had been so accepting of him that there was no reason to probe more deeply. Their public commitment was such that their personal differences seemed by comparison trivial, and were in any case overwhelmed by love.

Suddenly, she was now part of an alien world – the sophistries of Muslim politics, the dark secrets of the Indonesian military, the threat of other men. Was there another man, for whom all this spiritual transformation was merely a camouflage? Perhaps he had been a candidate in the elections, now destined for high office? There was a veil now between Indonesian history and politics and those who were active in them, and himself, who no longer had access to that world. He felt sad, desolate and afraid.

He lay on his bed, the room in darkness. Outside, the wind tossed the tops of trees wildly. Just across the corridor, she was lying on her bed. Her door was closed. Here she was, his wife, in their house, and he was not able to touch her. Or rather, he could touch her hand, she told him, but not hold it, certainly not squeeze it. He could kiss her on the cheek, but not the lips. He must not on any account lie on the bed with her or, if he did, he must be on the other side of the bed, out of touching range. She belonged now in some system devised by ancient Muslim male puritans (or perhaps, the thought occurred to him, a feminist Melbourne lawyer?). Once, they had welcomed each other into their different worlds and had shared a world of the future. The secular, humanist, democratic, transparent world order! Now all doors were shut and the future did not exist. She behaved as if she had been captured by a gang and brainwashed.

He still could not believe it was happening. He did not know who was lying in that bed in that room (which she had painted yellow, she said, because yellow made her feel at home). Her body must be the same, although how would he know? It was like armour, protecting everything she had once told him was held in sacred trust for him. And inside the body, the person was unrecognisable. She had been changed as if by magic potent, the creation of some art of alchemy, becoming steely, impenetrable, resolved. She, who was once among the most soft-hearted people in the world, who would break into tears at the sight of something beautiful or sad, a whale-watcher who would leap up and dive down with each movement of the sea animals, was now as tearless as an empty glass, as emotional as a matrix.

The more Mark tried to understand Rukmini, the more confused he became, leaving him with only one indisputable reality: she wanted to be rid of him.

The light under her door showed. He knocked and entered. She was wearing the green-blue dressing gown, her lower body under the bed cover she had brought from Sydney, orange and yellow sunflowers on a cream background. The sight of her thrilled and unnerved him. She was a serious student reading the Koran.

He sat on the end of the bed, beginning, as he thought, at the beginning. "When we were last together in Indonesia, I made plans, assuming that when the election was over and if there were a change of government and you wanted to be part of it, which I would fully understand and agree with, I would spend half the year in Jakarta. Your father had found space for a house for us on his block of land and an architect friend was drawing up plans. You remember? I was looking at investment possibilities and I had begun discussions with some university people about a research project on the cultural implications of globalisation, with one leg in Indonesia and the other in Australia. We exchanged e-mails and phone calls in the old affectionate way, right up until you were ready to come home. So when did this happen, this incredible change in you, so that, suddenly and without any warning, you treat me as if you never wish to see me again?"

He put a hand on his chest. "I am Mark. Remember me?"

As she made no reply, he continued. "You don't seem to have the slightest concern for the position you have put me in. Indeed, you behave as if it is my fault, that you are the victim of some mysterious circumstance of which I am the cause." He leaned across the bed. "If you do not wish to remember me as the person you loved, the person you taught that our love was sacred, the trust between us indissoluble, even after death, is it possible at least to treat me as a human being? I am a human being and I am crying out to you. Aren't you human, too? Is this you, this iron maiden, who cares for nothing except her own rights and interests? Is this really you?"

She listened to him, level-eyed, unflinching. "What is there to discuss. The marriage is over. There's nothing more to be said."

Mark had wondered if there was another hand in the letter, but he had to accept, facing her cold, appraising stare across the bed, the yellow room enclosing them like card players in a game to the death, no quarter offered or given, that the hand was hers, tested, perhaps, in circumstances of which he was hardly aware, but now under her own stern management as she plotted the course of her new life. He had thought that after a few days her mind might have cleared enough for her to realise that he did not stand in her way, that he welcomed the opportunity for her to serve her country. If she wished to convert to Islam, he would still love her. If she wished their children to be Muslim, he would not object. But she had arrived with an ultimatum. He had to meet steel with steel.

"My mind is clear on one point. I will not consent to a divorce, which you seem to regard as some kind of human right to which you are entitled. I will contest any application you might make. I have made this decision because I wish to defend our marriage, but also because of the arrogance with which you assume I should move aside so that you can go on to greater things."

"So now you're threatening me?" Her light voice quavered, pitched beyond its reach.

He stayed on familiar ground. "I am not threatening you. I am simply reminding you of the consequences of what you are doing. You want a divorce and you want it quickly. I am not going to oblige. The consequences are that you will have to wait and if you do have your moment in court, it may not be pleasant. You have a distinguished record, not only with me but among your friends, of contempt for those you chose to call 'the mussies.'"

"I've had enough of this."

She leaped out of bed so abruptly that he was bounced from its foot. She swept past him in a flurry of warm smells, turned off the overhead light, threw off her gown and, in her pink pyjamas, jumped back into bed (as he remembered her doing so often, quoting Sumi, her authority on pillow comfort). She flung out an arm to turn off the bed lamp, leaving him angry and trembling in the darkness.

"I keep telling you I need to get some sleep."

He placed a book of Matthew Arnold's poems at her door, with a yellow tab on the last verse of "Dover Beach".

Ah, love, let us be true
To one another! for the world, which seems
To lie before us like a land of dreams,
So various, so beautiful, so new,
Hath really neither joy, nor love, nor light,
Nor certitude, nor peace, nor help for pain;
And we are here as on a darkling plain
Swept with confused alarms of struggle and flight,
Where ignorant armies clash by night.

She did not respond and when he next came to her room, the book was lying on the floor.

16

They drove down the Great Ocean Road. The road clung to the side of wooded hills, glowing with sunlight and fresh leaves, dipping into a sea more green than blue, becoming purple in the distant ocean. The surf rolled soundlessly. The sky was high and light, transcending everything yet also seeming, as in a painting where form and content are one, to hold the world beneath in place.

Rukmini drove his car with her back upright, intent on shrugging off tailgaters, although traffic was light. In the old days, she would have been producing the view. He slouched, thinking, sometimes glancing hopefully at her determined profile. Since his bedside ultimatum, she had been more amenable. They had seen a film together, and when they had taken their seats in the cinema, she had allowed him briefly to hold her hand. Shopping together, she was her usual quick and competent self. The combination of Timor and the elections had kept Indonesia in the news: she was asked by ABC television news for an interview, which she gave, decorously covering her head in a lace shawl. Friends, including Patricia, rang to inquire if that was Rukmini on the telly with something on her head.

He had suggested Lorne, knowing that she loved it and hoping that it might kindle a spark of what he now thought of as the old Rukmini. It would be a cold, clear night and the stars would be out. "And at night the wondrous glory of the everlasting stars," he recited. He would get out the telescope! He would show her how the Southern Cross actually pointed to the south. Did she know the Milky Way was two hundred billion times the mass of the sun?

"I think stars are spooky," Rukmini said.

Now, in the car, she adopted a studied silence, against loud renderings of her favourite tapes and disks, such as Sade (especially "Woman of Somalia"), Enya and Kiri te Kanawa's "Songs of the Auvergne". As they left Geelong, Mark decided to break the ice.

"So you don't want to be Indonesia's Aung San Suu Kyi?"

She ignored him, humming along with Enya.

As they passed through Anglesea and began to glimpse the bright blue patches of sea that always lifted his spirits, he tried again.

"If we had had children, perhaps none of this would have happened."

He was trying to touch her emotions, while being careful not to apportion blame. That they had not become parents was one of those things, like missed business opportunities, he attributed to providence and a busy lifestyle, not to either of them personally.

"Alright, rub it in. I got the dates wrong."

Approaching Aireys Inlet, he tried again. "Perhaps it would have been different if we had not married."

She pulled the car to a screeching stop. "Are we having a nice drive to Lorne or are we having one of those discussions that never end?"

When they finally arrived in Lorne, she drove to a café on the pier they had liked because it was near a fish shop run by a poet whose weekly sonnets, scrawled on a sheet of paper posted on his shop window, were about lost love on the left bank of the Seine (although he was an emigrant from Greece). Before they left the car, she announced she would need to return to Melbourne early the following morning for an appointment, and then went straight to the café, ignoring the latest sonnet, which Mark lingered to read.

It was still about love on the left bank of the Seine, but it had lost (or was he imagining?) its romantic flavour, the assumption that men and women were engaged in a tango of energy and beauty in which rejection was as graceful as an embrace. Now, rejection had an air of finality, with a touch of cynical humour that had an Australian grain in it.

Crossing the Arafura Sea

Rukmini had taken a table at the far end, overlooking the sea, and he remembered he had once imagined, with her long hair and luminous skin, that she was a mermaid who might at any moment dive into the water, emerging on a rock to sing haunting songs of longing and desire. Now, she was an upright figure, with cropped hair, neatly folded scarf and buttoned jacket hiding all evidence of desire, holding with both hands a menu that apparently contained an item of food she was prepared to eat, and about which she was instructing a small, bowed figure at her side.

The evening passed in a cavalcade of empty gestures, without the stimulus of wine or coffee. Rukmini had decided that she would enjoy her meal, which she did by examining minutely each fork-lift of barbecued fish and masticating each morsel as if only distantly aware of the need to swallow it. Mark had decided that, as a last resort, he had nothing to lose with humour. "Life is short, so eat dessert first," he announced. He had seen it on the window of a café and now, an obedient servant of its philosophy, ordered strawberries and cream.

It was a relief for each of them to return to the car. When they reached home, she went to her bedroom and closed the door. There were three bedrooms and she chose the main one, which she and Mark usually shared. For a while he watched a cricket match on the other side of the world, and then went outside to see the stars. It was a clear night and the stars were, indeed, wondrous. He set up the telescope on the main deck, reciting galactic data to himself.

In the second bedroom, he was pursued in a dream by what he imagined was the Sea Goddess, or perhaps Rukmini's father in drag. Awake, he was assailed by the thought that the boyish, racist colonel in Jakarta might be the intended father of Rukmini's Muslim children. He turned on the radio, wondering what had happened in the world while he and his alienated wife were inflicting pain on each other. Were the futures markets up or down? Was anything being made of that intriguing remark by an international banker in Geneva that there was more money in disarming than in arming? How many had been killed in the Gaza Strip? Anything new on Timor? What was the state of play at the international meeting on "unwanted refugee flows", not to mention in the Test match he had been watching?

But the morning sun was awakening the birds, who responded by calling to each other and chasing about in the trees, reminding him that a day was waiting to be filled with human activity.

He regularly brought Rukmini breakfast in bed, even now. She always accepted it without protest, although she rejected like lightning any other move that might remotely be construed as compromising or conciliatory. After knocking lightly on the door, he entered carefully, preceded by the breakfast tray, held aloft. She was already awake, lying flat, staring at the ceiling. He helped her bunch up some pillows to cushion her back and she mumbled some kind of thanks. He drew back the curtains and raised the blind and she did not object.

"Did you get some sleep?" he inquired, like a dutiful husband.

"A bit."

As they sat primly over their coffee mugs, he mentioned that he had been wakened by the birds and that it promised to be a sunny day. She looked out the window and nodded, adding, in a neutral tone of voice, "I mustn't forget to check about that appointment."

He told her there had been a development on Timor. She nodded. "It doesn't change my view. Australia has betrayed the Indonesian people."

Was it too much to hope that the tangled skein of East Timor might provide material for a conversation?

"The Indonesian government perhaps, but not the people. And not the people of East Timor."

"You changed policy. And now you're ganging up against us."

This was the most she had said for days.

"Part of the international Jewish conspiracy?" he inquired, hoping to pierce with irony her memory of that dinner with the boyish colonel. But he pushed his luck too far, and he had forgotten the effect on her of early morning coffee.

"That's your interpretation," she said, getting out of bed and heading for the bathroom.

Mark drove on the return journey. Rukmini was quiet but after they had negotiated the roundabout at Anglesea and had stopped at the Freshwater Creek tearoom so that Mark could buy a hummingbird sponge, she suddenly spoke.

"Timor was unlucky to be colonised by both the Dutch and the Portuguese." She briefed Mark. The Portuguese had hung on for too long in the eastern half. They had been there since 1520. The Dutch had arrived in 1613. They had fought, dividing Timor between them in a treaty in 1860. "The Timorese have no reason to thank the Portuguese, who neglected them when they were not exploiting them, but now, because the West is powerful, some Timorese Christians are tugging the forelock." She shifted in her seat and straightened her shoulders. "There's some that are Catholics first and Timorese second. They're against the Indonesians because we're Muslim."

She appealed to Mark. "You don't know how lucky you are. You only had the English. And you've got this one, big country where everyone's the same."

"But not enough people to cover it properly," said Mark. "We should change places. You've got too many people on too many islands."

Rukmini was not impressed with ironic speculation. "Most of them are poor and most of you lot are well off."

From Geelong to Melbourne, she embarked on a history of religion and political power, which she had obviously been giving a lot of thought. Christianity began as a rebellious Jewish voice against the politically powerful Roman Empire. Christianity then became the religion of Rome and of Europe. The religion of Europe, colonialism and the powerful West was now, on half a small island in a Muslim archipelago, again the religion of the oppressed. But (with raised finger for emphasis) with a powerful Christian neighbour, who is doing all it can to make sure that this tiny half-island does not become Muslim like Indonesia."

"There's Singapore and Papua New Guinea, Thailand, Cambodia and Vietnam, the Philippines," said Mark. "None of them is Muslim."

But she would not be distracted from the irreducible fact that were it not for the twists and turns of colonial history, Timor would be one island and one people within the Indonesian archipelago and Australia had shown it was no friend of Indonesia's by not accepting that. On that note, he delivered her to the apartment.

"Let's continue this interesting conversation tonight. Would you like to go out for dinner?"

"Alright," she said. It was the longest conversation they had had since her return to Australia.

During the day, he argued back and forth in his head, convincing himself by lunchtime that when the full reality of what she was doing was laid out calmly, she would drop her icy resolve and talk to him as a human being capable of reason and understanding.

Tiresome calculations of marginal profit and loss in a fledgling company became important again. The drab streetscape and bedraggled city skyline suddenly revealed a hidden beauty – a romantic niche here, a soft glow of colour there. On the way home in early evening, he bought some pink and yellow roses, not red, which would be provocative; he would not present them, he would place them unobtrusively in a vase on the hallway stand, where she would be guided to them by their perfume. Strap-hanging in a tram, with the roses held tightly with his other arm, people, downcast for days, were alive and companionable again.

He paused with his key over the lock. He remembered other evenings with his key poised like this, light streaming onto the front porch, a faint smell of food, muffled sounds of music, the blurred colours of flowers through mottled glass. When he entered, she was not there to greet him. The apartment, dark and quiet, had an empty feeling. He switched on a light, called her name, went upstairs. Her pyjamas were strewn on her bed, her dressing gown thrown over a chair, her slippers upside down on the floor. So she had not yet returned.

Her little car was in the garage. He wandered into the kitchen, uneasy, and saw a small piece of folded paper secured to the bench by a pepper pot.

"The journeys of winter and summer do not meet. I have left for Jakarta. Take care. Rukmini."

17

HIS RECOVERY WAS SLOW. SO much of his success in business had come from his ability to get up each morning with the confidence that whatever he was intending to do that day was important in the general scheme of things. He still rose early, had breakfast, listened to the news, read newspapers, but sometimes he could not face the day and went back to bed, not to sleep, although he needed it because he would lie awake at night for long stretches with his eyes closed. He set in place a routine designed to keep himself busy with manageable tasks, but the business had developed a life of its own. The managers he had appointed were pleased to demonstrate their competence, leaving him with little to do. He spent hours staring into the distance, wondering about the future.

He had tempered the impact of the first shock, thinking that her e-mail might have been a clumsy joke, and then, if not, wondering why she was coming to Melbourne to discuss whatever it was. Her presence, although resolutely negative, offered glimmers of hope each day. The second shock was less of a surprise but more telling. He had stumbled to a chair and sat with the piece of paper and the pepper pot in his hands. He could not remember later whether he ate that night, or even whether he slept. All he knew was that she had come back, checked her bearings, tested her emotions and fled, wanting nothing more to do with him.

She had left her things all over the apartment and he did not move them. In her bedroom were her pink pyjamas, thrown on an unmade bed, her padded, green-blue dressing gown half-hung on the back of a chair, her blue slippers, soles up on the floor, just as she had left them. Rukmini liked comfortable shoes which were also stylish, showing off her slender ankles and delicate toes; she preferred brown leather walking shoes and her house shoes were a plait of mixed colours, half-heeled, one pair in a weave of taupe and beige, the other in a gold leather combination. Occasionally she wore heels, never spikey, invariably black satin, with thread-like straps. Something would have to be done with the shoes, but he could not decide what it was. They remained in a pile at the bottom of the wardrobe. Her car? Friends advised him to give it away, as they advised him to send her things and memorabilia back to her, or give them to charity. But he kept her little white car, driving it as often as possible in preference to his large blue sedan.

Her mail continued to arrive and was carefully put aside. Telephone callers were informed without amplification that she was in Jakarta. He brought out for scrutiny every relic of their time together. He examined old taxation returns, pored over airline tickets and hotel bills, diaries, noting every entry of his name, her address books, her notebooks, conference papers, albums of family photographs. He opened every perfume bottle and powder box, unwound every lipstick holder, tested every spray, sniffed at the scented sachets, the soaps, the lavender sprigs she had placed strategically, opened her sewing box with its cascade of buttons. Her clothes were left hanging, her underclothes remained in drawers. A trunk of traditional Indonesian costumes and hair arrangements, a pile of hats, her winter jackets and coats in the downstairs closet, all were touched by him with love and longing, forcing to the surface memories of their time together. He could not help himself, even when he knew how painful it would be.

Something would remind him of her and he would have to leave company abruptly, exiting with his shoulders heaving. In aircraft over Sydney's eastern beaches, he would remember her yellow house and break into barely controllable sobs. In their favourite coffee shops, he sat taut and unseeing, unable to order, his heart in turmoil. Driving in the countryside, he would sight a farmhouse, low to the ground and spread with gardens, secure and comfortable against the horizon, and he would have to pull off the road while he grappled with the memory that he would happily have lived with her in a house like that for the rest of his life.

A scene repeated itself. She tells him that she thinks her telephone is bugged. He is scornful, telling her to recruit the buggers into the secular, humanist, democratic, transparent world order. She kisses him passionately. "I love it when you say that ... I think you're glorious!"

When he walked in parks and gardens, or even in city streets, he would stop at the sight of flowers beginning to bloom or a budding tree, or a scent wafted across his path and he was suddenly desolate. One day in the botanical gardens, rhododendrons reared above him, purple, cherry, crimson, cardinal, magenta red, and he remembered strolling with her on this very path. "They're stunning!" He was pierced with tenderness when he smelled her roses.

"You must give her space to sort herself out." And, "She will come back in her own time." And, "She'll find out soon enough that military politics is no place for a woman." And, "Perhaps the move to Melbourne was too much – she was always a Sydney girl."

That's what some of her women friends were saying, but he didn't believe them. She had gone. From the moment she wrote the first letter until she left, she had behaved consistently. Occasional words that filled him with hope were just a delaying tactic, stalling his determination to understand and resolve. She wanted nothing more to do with him. She did not show any feeling, did not treat him as a human being, because she did not care for him. Perhaps she did not trust herself? Who could tell? The nuances were not important. What was important was her clear intention to rid herself of him and embrace a new life. How she did it depended on reserves of courage (in facing him) and cleverness (in deceiving him) and of the contingencies of Indonesian politics.

The family sighed and resigned itself to another chapter in the life of the money monk. "Here we go again." His sister sent a card: "Sorry to hear of the matrimonial upset." His mother told him that in stressful times she had always found it a relief to change the curtains. Patricia with the gleaming teeth sent him a page of instructions, including changing the locks, keeping a record of all communications with the former partner, forwarding mail unopened, cancelling joint bank accounts and getting a good lawyer.

"You need something to get you going," she said. She was like a doctor musing over a patient. "With most men, it's very simple. All they want is ... well, you can guess. Blow off the cobwebs! Break the logjam! Let off steam!" In a lah-di-dah voice: "Relieve the tension, dahling! But with some men, it's all in their heads. They need something to turn them on and once that happens, they're happy."

She introduced him to a friend, Nadia, an older woman with a head of bronze hair that glistened around a pale, intelligent face. She was a widow with two children, an eight-year-old boy and a girl a year younger. Their father had been killed in a car accident and Nadia was now trying to regain her place in the crowded legal profession. Nadia practised a studied air of dignity and reserve, as if she wished to suggest that she was not what it seemed, although she fluffed out her hair and twirled strands of it in a suggestive manner. Mark had known of her husband, and the accident in which he died had been well publicised. He appreciated Patricia's concern but Nadia and her two children were such a complete and identifiable package that he could not summon either the interest or the courage to open it.

Male business associates, especially those with a European background, were not impressed with Asian women. "They have their own ways. You're lucky to be rid of her. It's a shock at first, but in time you'll see it's a blessing in disguise."

The behaviour of Indonesia over East Timor had soured Australian public opinion and he set out to show that he was no longer captive to the political correctness of being nice to Asians. He stood back from the new world order of democracy and the rule of law. The trouble was, as soon as you identified a promising trend in global governance, a tin-pot dictator in Latin America, backed by the military, or a medieval bigot in the Middle East, backed by the mullahs, or a fearsome bully in Africa, swollen with lust and adorned with jewellery, would proclaim their right to a role in it. He began to think that Australians, with their democratic instincts, love of nature and leisure and their innocent longing for a good life, were a more hopeful guide to the future of life on planet earth than anyone else.

He would have felt easier in his mind if he could have blamed her, and, in a display of moral indignation, banished her. It would have been more dignified if he were able to put her and all she stood for out of his life, making it publicly clear that he had no respect for her. She had behaved badly. She had shown herself to be weak and ambitious. He saw her again sitting up in bed reading the Koran. She was a convert, in awe of her new religion, needing to justify the decision she had made, but incapable of sustained devotion. Her conversion was just a means to an end, establishing herself with the new political forces in Indonesia. She was not religious. If she had been born into Islam and had grown up within it, a return to the fold would have been conceivable. But she was, like her father, a believer in old Java, pre-Hindu, pre-Buddhist, pre-Christian, pre-Muslim, scornful of those who wanted to turn Indonesia into an Islamic state.

He wrote to the father by airmail, after deliberating for days on the form of address:

My dear Haryo,

Rukmini has said she wants to become a practising Muslim, have a Muslim marriage and Muslim children. Obviously, I cannot provide her with these. But if she wishes to find a Muslim father for her children, there is nothing I can do to stop her. As I understand it, for a true Muslim our marriage was never valid.

The law in Australia is that if there is mutual consent, a divorce can be managed without nastiness and publicity, although it can still take some time. Without consent, Rukmini will have to establish grounds for divorce. There are no grounds. I have been faithful to her in every respect, sexual, emotional, financial, political – the list can be stretched indefinitely. We have failed each other from time to time in lack of sensitivity and understanding, but nothing even lawyers could build a case on.

I would greatly appreciate any advice you may be able to provide on this distressing matter. In its own way, our marriage was a contribution to relations between Indonesia and Australia.

An additional reason for sadness is that I may not now have the opportunity to explore your philosophy of life. I remain, however, your admirer, even more so knowing that I have placed a burden on you by writing this letter.

Yours sincerely

Mark Chandler

Writing the letter gave him some satisfaction. He calculated that the father would not have been pleased by his daughter deserting the old religion of Java for new-fangled Islam, although he would balance that with pride and hope of a future in politics (if that is what she intended) and the relief of removing a son-in-law who did not believe in the Sea Goddess. He did not know what he was asking for and did not even expect a reply, but the letter connected him with someone close to Rukmini on the other side of the Arafura Sea. She could remove herself from his world, but she could not exclude him from hers.

A response from the father, also by airmail, came surprisingly quickly.

Dear Chandler,

Your letter came to me. My daughter's behaviour can be puzzling at times, but she has not lost sight of her country's destiny. It would not be good for Indonesia if Muslim sharia law on marriage was accepted, so she is seeking a divorce according to secular law. Whether she will be content, if she is successful, is a question only the future can answer. What you call my philosophy of life is to accept its great variety. Relations between Indonesia and Australia are part of that variety. I wish you well in your business affairs.

Haryo

While it was hardly substantial, the father's elusive acknowledgement of the situation gave Mark a flicker of hope. Haryo's detachment was never explained, let alone justified, but it was always there, reassuring. Human attachments, like family and friends, rivals and enemies, needed to be kept in their place, somewhere in the lower order of things. The agony and the ecstasy would pass; what remained was a higher consciousness. You had to learn how to live in the body, have family and friends, enjoy life while not becoming so attached that when the inevitable occurred, like death (or divorce), it was insupportable.

Mark wondered if he should try to think like Haryo or, more comfortably in his own culture, scientifically. Scientists were able to live with uncertainty because they had a firm grip on first principles. If things did not behave in an expected manner, scientists did not change their way of thinking. They looked for an explanation, confident that they knew where and how to look. They were not dismayed and disillusioned when they did not find what they wanted. They just kept looking. If you examined the constitutions the nations of the world had produced to explain who they were, you found references to religion, human rights, education, health and even happiness, but not to the scientific method as the instrument of true knowledge. Governments upheld the separation of church and state, vowed to make their economies truly competitive, but nothing was done to make sure that the citizens of a democracy had the benefits of scientifically tested information when they voted. Perhaps scientific thinking, not the secular, humanist, transparent new world order, was the answer.

In a mood of detachment, he decided it was time to put a shine on his shoes. He brought out a worm-eaten box containing polish, a variety of brushes and cleaning rags, as well as bundles of shoelaces. He recovered from the depths of a wardrobe a range of shoes, black and brown, and set to work.

He speculated on the hold that shoes seemed to have on the human imagination. A Chekhov character, thought to be English because his shoes were polished, came to mind; Russians wore boots that were always dirty. Women's shoes were enshrined in erotica. He had read a magazine article that argued that a man's shoes, next to his ties, revealed what sort of person he was, or at least what sort of person he wanted others to think he was, which was a good indication of the sort of person he truly was if you worked on the assumption that he was a vastly different person from the one he wanted everyone to think he was. The writer had deduced (no research involved) that authoritarian minds were attracted to brogues.

There were other signs of recovery. He accepted social invitations. In the mornings, he went downstairs early to get the newspapers, and then read them with breakfast, as he used to do, instead of taking them back with him to bed. He tended Rukmini's roses. He supported, even to the extent of writing letters to the newspapers, a campaign to allow ashes of the dear departed to be scattered in the Royal Botanic Gardens. He wrote calmly, with old-fashioned eloquence, that if it was legal to bequeath a seat from which future generations could view the gardens' delightful vistas, it should be legal to nourish the soil that sustained their floral beauty (and, incidentally, save money on fertilisers). Lovers of the gardens rose up as one, declaring that burnt human remains were bad for the plants, and squeamish citizens said the idea gave them the shivers ("Makes Flesh Creep" said a headline).

He could not be detached from the little things of life for long or he ceased to feel alive, so he set out to pay attention to everyday events. He stopped to examine a bird sitting on a fence, not because he was interested in how it perched but because he wished to pay attention to an everyday occurrence. He looked with intensity at each item on a shelf in a convenience store, not because he was checking before buying or because he was interested in a particular product in comparison with what was available in another store, a bakery or a chemist, but because he wished to acknowledge the singular identity of the product and the design and marketing skills that made it accessible to the public. He walked at night, peeping at people in their illuminated rooms. In daylight, he scrutinised their clothing. Some men wore cufflinks that glistened. Some women wore spike-heeled shoes with toes like the bows of kayaks. He halted outside crowded restaurants, watching people eating so closely together they could, if they wished, feed each other. He studied paintings he did not like, but were reputed to be interesting. He read books he had no desire to read but felt compelled by word of mouth to investigate.

But the hold she had over him would not go away. His personal and public lives were so intertwined that he could not consider his attitude to public issues without thinking of her. He came slowly to appreciate that if he were to apply himself again to business, he had to stop thinking that he had been betrayed by her and that she should be punished. He was on the brink of understanding that, obliged to chose between her two countries, she had chosen the one for which she felt she had more to give. From the point of view of raising a family, she might even be more comfortable in Indonesia, with domestic support. Schools and hospitals were a worry, but you could manage if you had money or political influence.

Then an e-mail arrived, sending him back to bed to stare at the ceiling. Now he wondered whether despite her vows of undying devotion, she had ever really loved him.

Dear Mark,

Things are difficult enough without bringing my father into it. The time has come for me to tell you what really happened.

I fell in love with another man, and I could not bear to tell you. I knew you would be devastated. So I had to let you down gently. And, in a way, it is a religious and political matter because he is a religious and political person. So everything is connected, and I feel for the first time in my life that everything fits with everything else, my love for him, my country and my God. I cannot tell you what a wonderful feeling it is. I was born here. These are my people. I know now what I have to do with my life. You remember how I used to say poverty was Indonesia's great problem. Well, I am working with the poor, providing things like food, clothing and shelter. I was always embarrassed when Australia and other Western countries felt they had to provide Indonesia with money for basic things. Surely we can do this ourselves. The people are restless and if something isn't done, the crazies will take over.

I accept that our marriage was my doing. I did not scheme and calculate. I just opened your eyes to what loving someone was like and it worked. It changed you. You learned how to open up, go with the flow. And I wanted marriage because that was your return gift to me. It showed that you took me seriously as a person. Actually, I did not expect you to marry me. I thought, when push came to shove, you would not take the next step. I was too light and airy for you, too frivolous. And, although you behaved like a European gentleman, I suspected you might be an Aussie boy at heart. I loved the freedom in Australia, but it scared me, too. You got it from Europe but in Australia it runs wild, like the prickly pear, the rabbit and the cane toad.

I wondered about our children growing up as Australians, because the prospects for them were so much better than here. That bothered me.

Anyway, we didn't have them, which at the time depressed me but now it seems like a stroke of good luck.

When I came down to Melbourne I thought I could be honest with you. But it didn't work. I should have told you the truth. As Sumi used to say, you have to be cruel to be kind. But you were so upset, I just couldn't. And I couldn't stay either. If I'd stayed another day I would have given in, just to ease the pain. Or jumped off the roof. Remember Lake George! And that would have been terrible for both of us, and for this other person.

I just fled from the house. I walked until I found a taxi and told him to drive me to the airport. I took only a few precious things, like my grandmother's jewellery from that hidden cupboard in the kitchen where we kept leftover foreign currency from trips (I didn't take any money). The flights to Indonesia had left, so I took the first to Sydney and flew on to Jakarta the next day.

I'm sorry for all this trouble but I hope, now that you know the truth, that you will understand and let me live the life I want here. Our time together was precious and important for me. But the rest of my life has to be here, with someone else.

Take care,

Rukmini

He printed the letter and read it again and again. It was an honest letter, written without protective care of her trumpeted rights and interests should it ever be produced in court. To his surprise, he found it easier at first to think of her with another man than as a religious convert. When they were together, the thought of another man, even in the past, had been unbearable, but now he knew that she was gone, it was more convincing than her conversion to Islam, although (he warned himself) perhaps that was because the man was as yet an abstraction. Who was he? Someone in politics apparently, probably in her group around the new president. He shrugged.

He slipped back into thinking about politics the way he used to think before he encountered Rukmini. He had always thought love and the market had much in common. She had thrilled him with her declarations of undying love, but in real life whether something lasted depended on the balance between supply and demand. The market was as relentless as love in its judgments, but it was easier for human beings to deal with, making their own decisions in the hope of outwitting it. The rough and the smooth. Win some, lose some.

Was she merely a creature of circumstance and contingency? They had been thrown together by chance and the sparks had flown. She had been excited by the interest shown by a mature Australian man, representing material security and the liberal values of the West, triumphant in the Cold War. She set out to arouse him sexually. She probably had a colourful view of sexual behaviour in Western societies and was anxious to impress.

Was their time together, their determination to expose themselves honestly and fully to each other, the family farm and the Pacitan clan, the marriage in Prague, *The Bus Ride to Canberra*, *Remember Lake George!*, *The Seduction at Tanjung Priok* and *The Turning of ASIO* not signposts on a road map to love that would last – and the creation of a new world order – but merely the fanciful embroidery of an affair?

Depressed, he studied death notices and read obituaries, presenting himself at the funerals of people he had not known. The obituaries were glimpses of history, not just personal narratives, tragically interrupted or nicely fulfilled. Sometimes history and politics triumphed, sometimes love found a way, sometimes ambition was indomitable against the odds. He wondered how his own obituary would be written. He noted the social standing of people at funerals, the size of the gathering and the kind of service, whether religious or secular, whether formal or communal, the selection of speakers, the participation of families. What colleagues and partners said was often repeated in the media, but was often not as interesting as the contribution of grandparents and children. "The old and the young do not bother with propriety," he told himself.

He read "Dover Beach" again, and it seemed now like a lament for a lost world, not a lost love. The human race had taken leave of its senses. He had thought that people were peaceful by nature, that only governments wanted war. But all over the world, people could not wait to get at each other's throats. If governments made them do it, they performed in a more organised and efficient way, but they wanted to do it anyway.

People did not want to be civilised. They wanted to be themselves, meaning nasty. They did not want to be better than animals. They wanted to be more like animals, worse than animals, killing their own. They did not want to rise above their differences. They wanted to sharpen their differences, wallow in them, kill and maim each other because of them. Wherever he looked, he saw disorder and depravity. The world was a disgusting place.

He marvelled at the wealth and expertise expended on activities that are inessential, while millions of people are exhausted with poverty and disease. The exquisite crafting of jewellery and the seductive designing of cars, for example. Opera: the music, the voices, the sets. The sport of kings: a global industry in breeding and training horses and in finding small, strong men to ride them, in deciding pedigrees, names and colours, in building racecourses, devising betting systems, calculating odds. Was this civilisation? Or was it deciding to have a public holiday on the day of a horse race? In Melbourne during the racing season women decked themselves in eccentric hats and dresses. Was that civilisation? Or was it civilised not to be offended by them nor to pity them, but to be moved by them later, sitting tipsy in trams, their feet bare, as if they had given up trying to be stylish and were now themselves? People packed themselves into cities, living in buildings like anthills, choking streets with cars. Animals were force-fed and battery-prodded to produce more food at cheaper prices. Was that civilisation? The stock exchange. Casino capitalism.

What was civilisation? Libraries and museums, mansions and cathedrals, orchestras, the civil service, professional ethics? Was public health and education a measure of it, or wealth and power? Was it civilised to allow abortion, to permit homosexuals to marry and to decriminalise the use of marijuana? Or was that the thin end of the wedge, the start of a slippery slope? He remembered Rukmini defending the unborn foetus. Yet so many who were against abortion on the grounds that life was sacred, wanted to kill others because they had different beliefs from their own.

He knew that if he remained true to his declaration that he would defend his marriage in the courts, he could rely on anti-Indonesian public sympathy in Australia. She had gone over to the other side. He could draw on evidence in her e-mails and her behaviour to show that she was not the victim of nefarious Australian influences, not forced against her will to cohabit with a non-believer, not required to prostitute herself to the pernicious cultural, economic and political forces of the society she had adopted for the understandable, if misguided, objective of gaining a technically efficient education and a job. She was in love with him, as he was with her, and she was devoted to Australia, suspicious of militarists and Islamists, happy in her marriage and confident of the future. It would all come out in court.

He replied to a letter from Rukmini's Sydney lawyer, agreeing to a divorce, arranged for her clothes to be given to a charity, sold her little car, and started thinking again about the future of his business.

18

WHEN THE AMERICANS EXPLODED IN fear and anger after the terrorist attacks on the World Trade Centre in New York and the Pentagon in Washington, Mark Chandler declined to be associated with warnings that the war on terrorism was a religious crusade and anti-terrorist legislation being proposed, and copied by Australia, would infringe civil liberties and threaten human rights. When the Bali bombings brought political terrorism to Australia's doorstep, he tried to get in touch with her, but she didn't respond to calls on her mobile, text messages or e-mail. According to the newspapers, a shadowy Indonesian organisation called Jemaah Islamiyah, affiliated with Al Qaeda, was responsible. As the figures were confirmed, 202 people killed, including 88 Australians, and 320 others injured, he succumbed to improbable twinges of guilt.

He saw them standing together on the headland overlooking the surf beach at Pacitan. He saw her straight back, her long black hair, slender neck, her tender face turned towards him. He imagined again the Javanese fortress from which they would guide the fortunes of the clan, even the nation. Together, they would be invincible, symbols of a greater good in which others could share. The thread of their marriage would hold their two nations in place, binding them together even when forces within wanted to split them apart.

She, not he, had broken the spell. Still, he felt guilty. If they had stayed together, perhaps there would have been no Bali bombings, no broken bodies, no screams of pain and howls of rage, no religious taunting across the waters. Whose side was she on now? He had never believed she could be a good Muslim, but was it possible she had become a bad one? He realised with a shock that it was easier to imagine her as a bad Muslim than a good one. He researched the Internet, fearing that her name would suddenly jump out at him.

He had often been to Bali, but he had never been to the Sari Club and nearby Paddy's Bar. The young Australians who had died in them were part of a pleasure-seeking invasion of the island that he and Rukmini tried to avoid. They chose secluded locations in the west and north of the island. She regarded Denpasar as a trinket of international tourism, not part of real Indonesia, and he regarded the Australians who went there on holidays as adolescent, like the schoolies who flocked to Australian resorts at the end of the year to celebrate freedom from education.

On impulse, when the trial of the alleged Bali bombers was announced, he booked a room in their favourite hotel in Candidasa, knowing that he could drive to Denpasar in an hour and a half if he wished to attend the trial. He knew he would not be able to resist and on the day the trial opened, he sat in the handsome, traditional court building, with vaulted ceiling of brown wood, supported by cantilevered stone pillars and tall glass walls through which he could see the orange and red tiles and leafy foliage of old Bali, far from the razzmatazz of Kuta.

Amrozi, one of three brothers on trial, was a cheerful man with a perpetual smile. A slight figure in a pale apricot shirt, he was overwhelmed by the building itself and the black robes and vermilion silk of the judges, but not overawed by them, nor, apparently, by the prospect, if found guilty, of facing a firing squad. He seemed pleased with his role in the bombings. He agreed that he had delivered six hundred kilograms of potassium to Denpasar from his hometown Lamongan, near Surabaya. He also accepted that his van was in the vicinity when the bombings occurred. His defence seemed to be that the chemicals he transported could not have caused such a massive explosion.

The Indonesian legal system is inquisitorial, based on the Napoleonic code, not adversarial like the Australian system, so there was no cross-examination. The five judges (one a woman) would have to make up their own minds about Amrozi's credibility. However, he left them in no doubt about his opinion of the Sari Club and Paddy's Bar, and the people who went there. They were dens of iniquity, corrupting Indonesian youth and undermining the integrity of the Indonesian nation. Mark had in his pocket a glossy brochure, extolling the benefits of high fashion and exclusive travel, and describing Kuta as "a nasty fleshpot of cheating, dope, prostitution and crime". It could have been written by Amrozi.

During a break, he mixed with Australian families – mothers and fathers, brothers and sisters, attending the trial because a member of their family had been in the Sari Club or Paddy's Bar on the fateful night. They were from all over Australia, but especially from centres of the Australian game of football, Perth and Melbourne. A couple from Perth, who had lost their son with, it seemed, half his team, were there as a gesture of remembrance, but also to see that their son and his mates received justice. It was not clear how they intended to do this. They had no knowledge of Indonesia and, as they did not speak the language, no understanding of what was happening in the court, but they had sat stoically throughout the proceedings, following the story by watching the faces, as if at a pantomime. They now clustered around a diplomat from the Australian embassy answering their questions and providing a commentary on proceedings in court.

Mark was reminded that Australia and Indonesia were probably the most dissimilar neighbours in the world, the forces of both history and geography having conspired to keep them apart. They were not only opposites physically – a large island continent and an archipelago – but also the natural erosion of differences that usually occurred with contiguity, creating overlaps of ethnicity, culture and religion, had not happened with Australia and Indonesia. So relations between the two countries depended on the two governments, who were sensible enough, preferring peace to conflict, but lacked any ballast of understanding and connections between the two peoples. Every now and then, a small incident would erupt, breaking what seemed like a smooth surface.

The bombings were a big incident, not a small one. Yet the unintelligible proceedings in a courtroom in Bali were a hopeful sign of integrity and calm in the counter-terrorism frenzy being played out in the rest of the world. This was not kill or be killed frontier justice, as was being undertaken in a replay of the Wild West in Afghanistan and Iraq. And a human tragedy was bringing Australians to Bali not for fun but to grieve.

He came home reassured that Australia and Indonesia were not about to become adversaries. The gulf of understanding across the Arafura Sea could be bridged. It was time to stop dreaming about what might have been with Rukmini and the new world order and face the practical challenge of making a success of business.

When he was with Rukmini, he believed that Australia had a role to play in the world. Now, he was reminded every day that Australia was still developing. It had a population of only 23 million, occupying territory about the size of Brazil, which had a population of 180 million. It was greater in size than India, which had more than a billion people. The population was clustered in the eastern states and was highly urbanised, copying the model of developed, industrialised societies. The centres of population were as far as possible from neighbours, with the exception of New Zealand. Once seen as security against invaders, the empty spaces between cities and neighbours now glared as a case of lopsided development. Western Australia was huge and manifestly unmanageable, physically the size of Queensland, New South Wales and Victoria combined. The Northern Territory, with Darwin offering itself as the gateway to south-east Asia, was not even a State. And Australia had a constitution that said it was governed by a vice-regal system and did not even mention the prime minister and cabinet.

The politicians were so anxious to snare the votes of people in the cities that they had lost the will to develop the rest of the country. What was needed was a new version of the Snowy Mountains project. He devised in his head a scheme in which recent immigrants and young Australians would be conscripted to form labour gangs in the outback, working on major development projects.

19

MARK SITS IN A CHESTERFIELD chair in a new office in a new building in the heart of Melbourne's central business district. The chair is the only reminder of the old jarrah and brass rooms where family business had been conducted from time immemorial. Two young men and a young woman produce a whiteboard, and then each a laptop, which they open on a glass-topped table.

The first young man's scribble is small and tight, like his voice. The second's presentation is sprawling, which he accompanies with a tale or two of workplace misdemeanours. The young woman's job is to inform the dominant shareholder that whether he had money to spend depended on how well other people managed the business. And, of course, the global financial situation.

Whenever one of them said "the global financial situation", the others solemnly nodded.

"I want to stay put and be global at the same time," Mark said.

They explained in triplicate that the answer in principle was Yes, while the answer in practice was No. It would be like turning around an ocean liner, or crash-landing a jet in a field. They demonstrated by whirling their outstretched arms in an ungainly fashion.

"The exploration of space – might that be possible?" Mark inquired courteously. "Australia, with its vacant space, is surely the perfect site. We should open our minds to the vast reality beyond our planet," he suggested, looking hopefully at each of the three in turn. They smiled without enthusiasm.

"Electric cars? Lithium?" They were immune to novelty and innovation.

"So what have we got?"

The whiteboard became a flowchart of arrows and circles, figures and names, intended to illustrate a message that the young woman delivered verbally, which was that the company's proposed acquisition of an interest in a gold and copper mine on the island of Sumbawa needed urgent attention. The deal had not been without complications (a feathered glance at her co-conspirators), Indonesian politics being unpredictable, but now that the political situation had been resolved, in a manner of speaking (the feathered glance became bolder), it was likely that approvals from various authorities would be forthcoming.

"How did all that get under the radar?" asked Mark, meaning how did the company's interest in the Sumbawa mine reach this point without him knowing.

"Derivatives," said one. "Forward contracts," said the other. "ETCs," said the young woman. She explained that you didn't need actually to own something in order to trade it. Gold, for example. You didn't need to possess gold bullion in order to sell it. What you possessed was an exchange-trade commodity or an ETC.

"I'd prefer the real thing," Mark said.

The young woman left the room. She returned holding a Royal Mail canvas bag, containing a weighty object, which she eased onto the glass-topped table, and then stood back in admiration. It was a gold bar.

"5.76 kilos," said one.

"Half a million dollars," said the other.

"Not frangible," said one. "Not frangible at all."

"But fungible," said the other. "Very fungible."

They were like recent graduates of a business school, where they had heard the words "frangible" and "fungible" for the first time.

"Solid," said one and the others nodded. "The global financial situation." They all nodded together, solemnly.

"As good as gold," said the young woman, allowing herself a laugh in the deadly serious pantomime.

At first, the bar of gold had seemed to Mark like a lump of pressed metal in the form of a large brick but now it was beginning to shine, as if appreciating what was being said about it.

"Why are we having this demonstration of gold's remarkable qualities?" he asked.

They explained that in the light of the global financial situation, and the effect of terrorism on the transport industry, investment in gold was a safe haven. There was also climate change, the effect of which on the economy was impossible (they raised hands in unison to indicate quotation marks and shouted "Politics!") to predict.

The young woman elaborated on gold's charming qualities. The building boom around the world, especially in China, had boosted the mining of iron ore, especially in Australia, but it could not go on forever. Gold did not depend on the construction of tall buildings, sporting arenas, railways and roads. It had a life of its own, in the imagination of people all over the world. Whatever the politicians and central bankers decided, whether oil, coal or solar power became the energy of the future, gold would always be marketable, always solid.

"Very solid," said her supporting chorus.

In short, the recommendation to the dominant shareholder was to turn the good ship Chandler away from the laborious and increasingly frangible industry of transport into the magical and fungible alchemy of gold. Mark sensed that a board decision was looming. He asked for particulars of the Sumbawa mine, which were provided instantly in the form of a glossy brochure and tax returns.

As he left the room, bowed out by the triumvirate, he could see the gold bar glowing on the glass table.

He remembered complaining that governments had gone off the Gold Standard so they could print their own money. Rukmini had listened without sympathy, fingering her rings. She loved gold. She would peer into the windows of jewellery shops, muttering about this or that carat. Inside, she pored over rings, holding them to the light, polishing them on her sleeve. She treasured a family wedding band her father had given her. He had spent hours in her wake, wondering what it was about the yellow metal that not only captivated her but held her in awe. She loved perfumes, too, but as adjuncts to her personality. Gold was something else, itself, somehow magical and mysterious, its lustre independent of the decorative arts with which people tried to tame it.

The Sumbawa mine would give him an excuse to be in Indonesia. From the point of view of Australian business in the Asian century that everyone was talking about, it would be an asset. Australia was open again for business. He would show the Indonesians how to make money. Also, he would be crossing the Arafura Sea into her world. For a while, he convinced himself that his new project would not only keep him busy, but make him happy.

But his life continued to feel empty without her. When he remembered the time when enchantment had filled every moment, he felt lonely and sad.

Every time he stopped for petrol, he remembered what it was like to be with her. As he listened to the liquid gurgling into the tank, he would catch a glimpse of the way her hair fell to her shoulders, and turned upwards, and he would marvel that she was there, sitting in his car. What was she thinking? Would she ask him to buy her something to drink or to eat? Should he ask her? Would she wish to visit the toilet and, if so, where was it? As he walked across to the main building to pay, the whole petrol station would be glowing, like a stage lit up. When he had paid and was returning to the car, the first glimpse of her face through the windscreen would overwhelm him with happiness.

There she was, waiting for him!

About the Author

AUSTRALIAN WRITER-DIPLOMAT BRUCE GRANT HAS written ten works of non-fiction, three novels, essays and short stories published in *The New Yorker*, *Mademoiselle*, *Playboy*, *Cleo*, *The Bulletin*, *Quadrant*, *Overland* and *Meanjin*. His first book, *Indonesia*, became a classic. *Crossing the Arafura Sea* is the third novel in a trilogy on the theme "Love in the Asian Century". He was a Nieman Fellow at Harvard University, Australian High Commissioner in New Delhi, foundation chairman of the Australia-Indonesia Institute, chairman of the Australian Dance Theatre, chairman of the Victorian Premier's Literary Awards, president of Melbourne's International Film Festival and president of Melbourne's International Arts Festival. His essay "The Great Pretender at the Bar of Justice", written at the trial of Slobodan Milosevic, was published in *The Best Australian Essays 2002*. "Bali: The Spirit of Here and Now", written after the October 2002 bombings, was published in *The Best Australian Essays 2004*. He was awarded the degree of Doctor of Letters (*honoris causa*) by Monash University in December 2003 and distinguished Fellow by the Australian Institute of International Affairs in 2010.

www.ingramcontent.com/pod-product-compliance
Lightning Source LLC
Chambersburg PA
CBHW051834020726
47502CB00005B/1785